RETURNEE

VERNELLA FULLER

Saint James, Jamaica
books@fruithillpress.com

A catalogue record for this book is available from the National
Library of Jamaica.

DEDICATION

To my late father, my mother and my daughter, Alisha.

CONTENTS

PREFACE

In characteristically expressive Jamaican parlance,
'returnee 'is the term used by the Jamaican
Government to describe citizens who – having resided
abroad – have chosen to move back to Jamaica.

Typically characterised as the 'reverse migration' of
those who left for the West in the 1950s and 60s,
actual returnees are a motley collection of those whose
birth, ancestry, marriage or good fortune have enabled
them to claim the fabled tropical inheritance that is
Jamaican citizenship.

The respectable cousin of Deportees*; the
phenomenon of returnees is interesting precisely
because these economically powerful, worldly and
dual-passport-holding Jamaicans have options that

extend – ostensibly at least – beyond the confines of a small, apparently struggling island. Indeed, the growing ranks of returnees speak of the complexity that notions of belonging, responsibility, identity, philanthropy and patriotism bring in a globalised, postmodern age.

Returnees are a minority group within Jamaican society whose cultures, accents, expectations and trappings differ starkly from those of the indigenous population, despite their 'common' heritage. Whether fulfilling the promise of their forebears to return, attempting to outwit more sophisticated legal and tax machinery, or simply luxuriating in paradise, returnees provide an unparalleled prism through which Jamaican culture can be examined.

Through her examination of returnees, Vernella Fuller's fascinating first-hand account provides a nuanced, uncompromising and at times uncomfortable insight into modern Jamaica.

* Deportees – those forcibly ejected from a country, typically for breaking the law, who presumably would prefer to renounce their Jamaican citizenship and stay in their foreign home.

Dr. Alisha Fuller-Armah

1 PARADISE

A friend from that other country was holidaying in Jamaica. He came to visit for a couple of days and joined us on one of our morning walks. He marvelled at the over 7000 acres of forest, golf courses, hills and valleys through which we walked.

DJ is an avid bird watcher and educated us about the woodpecker that paused momentarily to eye us before continuing to peck, peck, peck.... And the swarm of parakeet that NE was convinced we had seen grow from fledglings. I could not be sure, but humoured her and agreed. As if on cue, a swallow-tailed kite hovered and rested without a care on the peak of a queen palm.

We were about halfway around one of the four walks that we frequented, the one which led to a private beach. We had to go up a steep incline, down another, past the ruins of the old sugar mill and the naseberry trees where each dog always seemed to find a naseberry to devour, past the clubhouse, under the tunnel, over the bridge, through the meadow, to finally get to the beach. There we would sit for half an hour or so, perhaps even dip our feet in the water, or throw smooth, colourful pebbles in the shallow sections, away from the rocks, for the dogs to chase.

Someone had told us that the thicket bordering the dazzling white sand was a protected nesting ground for sea turtles. We were careful to keep our two dogs Impenzi and Pimlico, away.

Impenzi, our poodle Pekingese, although he is afraid of the waves, he loves chasing things. He will forget the most boisterous waves to fetch whatever is thrown, returning to wait with uncontrollable excitement for you to throw another. His brother Pimlico, wagging his glorious Pekingese Shih Tzu's tail blissfully cools his stomach in the water, uncaring of the waves. 'This place is like another country,' DJ said. 'It doesn't feel like we are in Jamaica.'

'How do you mean?' I asked.

'This is paradise,' he said.

I turned possible responses around in my head, knowing by experience that I had to be careful what I said. If I played down what is clearly sublime, if I did not use the superlatives he was convinced were suitable, he might judge me adversely. If I used the said superlatives, he might think me immodest.

Conversely, if I gave my reservations about aspects of life as I was experiencing it, he might think me ungrateful and impossible to please.

After all, when he had first seen our property, in true that other country style he had said, 'Not modest by any standard.' I had smiled broadly, loving his inimitable British way with words, and the equally unique sense of humour.

Fortunately now, while I was still pondering his question, other extraordinary things took our attention; an unknown bird, or fruits hanging invitingly from diverse trees. We marvelled at those, picking some to munch, regretful that others were not ripe enough and ignoring the weightier question of whether living in the lap of Mother Nature meant living in paradise.

Later still, unable to drag ourselves away to ramble homewards, we sat, eyes fixed on the impossible turquoise sea, the expanse of blue sky with its cumulus humilis clouds. I asked if he had had a chance to go around the island and whether he had taken notice of the place names, especially the informal ones. He had, and in character had taken notice.

'Interestingly,' I said, 'in the parish where I was born there is a place informally named Sufferers Heights, and near here there is one called Paradise.

The reality of being a returnee in Jamaica,' I added, perhaps with a tinge too much reflection, 'the reality of living here is somewhere between the two.'

2 PEAR TIME

I remember as a child marking the time of year both by the school terms and by the fruits that were currently in season. We used to call the seasons time; so we had mango time, guinep time, tangerine time, naseberry time, pear time, and so on. We all had our favourite seasons but one of mine was, without a doubt pear time.

Much later, when I had returned home from that other country, one of the contractors building our house asked me if I liked pier. It took me a few seconds to understand that he was referring to what I call avocado pear, or simply pear. I told him that I did, but he said nothing else. I put his non-response down as one of the many exchanges that I did not fully understand; one lost in translation. Or possibly it was his way of adding to his tally of judgments about this strange woman from foreign.

A week or so later he brought me a plant. 'Dis will be the sweetest pier you ever tasted,' he said.

Through my broad smile and profuse thanks, I asked him how long it would be before it bore fruit.

'About five years,' he said. That will be a lesson in deferred gratification, I thought.

Amidst the rubble of an unfinished house, and a rocky plot of land without topsoil, our gardener planted the young tree. The builders eventually finished the house, and the rocks and rubble disappeared under truckloads of top soil. Delightful plants with extraordinary colourful flowers and leaves burst through, magnificent fruit trees that we bought or that friends and family members donated. Small creatures made their habitat between them, feasting and dancing daily among them.

During the second year, a friend said casually,

'You'll need to crop the pear tree so it doesn't get too tall.' I asked our gardener if that was correct; he agreed, and in another week or so, I noticed that the topmost branches had been trimmed.

I did my daily walk around the garden admiring the wildlife, the vibrant colours, and varieties, picking herbs and fruit that were in season or collecting bags full of produce that the gardeners picked. More often than not, I gazed in awe. In such a short time, tiny saplings magically transformed into large trees bursting with vegetables, fruits, and herbs, with compliments of Mother Nature. I paid only fleeting attention to the pear tree, whose time had not yet come.

In year three, the gardener called me, 'You will be eating pear this year, you know. There are over a dozen on the tree.'

Amazed, I went with him to see. The tree was not as big as I had imagined it needed to be to bear fruits, or as strong as the pear trees I had known as a child in the hills of Saint Catherine. The branches looked juvenile; the leaves seemed sparse and were brownish-green, as there had been no rain for some weeks. Notwithstanding, there were pears on the tree. We carefully counted twenty tiny fruits. Excitedly I asked,

'When will they be ready?'

'A few months yet,' he said. I had learnt by then that the term few is a non-specific quantity, so I decided that I simply had to wait patiently and see.

A couple of months passed, 'Are they nearly ready?' I asked the gardener.

'It is best to let them drop,' he said, with a patient, knowing expression.

The pears grew steadily, despite the weeks of drought. My mother visited and I took her to see the tree, hoping she would say they were ready. She echoed the gardener's advice but confirmed it as a special variety that was not commonplace. She said she would have to return when they were ready so she could taste them.

Friends and other family members came and I took them to pay homage to the pear tree. The initiated echoed that it was indeed a rare variety.

I went to the tree at least twice a day, longing for the pears to drop. The supermarket and open markets overflowed with pears; friends called by with three, four, even a dozen pears that came from their own trees. I tried but could not resist them; pear with breakfast, pear with lunch, pear as a snack and pear with dinner. The most lethal combination and a childhood favourite were pear and ginger bulla cake, greedily devoured at any time of day. I increased my exercise level in the struggle to maintain my weight.

One day, impatient, I pulled down a limb and picked one of our own stubborn pears.

The gardener reprimanded me, 'Dat won't ripe for now. It not fit yet.'

Nature, though slow, was kind. Two weeks later after it had been carefully wrapped in newspaper and left in a dark cupboard, the unripe pear was transformed into a succulent, firm, and flavourful delight.

A few days later, I walked to the tree with the dogs, Pimlico and Impenzi, and found two overripe pears on the ground filled with ants. When did that happen?

Was that how it was going to be? It was then that I realised that the dogs loved pears too. They grabbed one of the fallen pears each and bounded down the garden with them.

Later, others fell but were too damaged for us. As if and eat them with relish, ripe or unripe. I took to going earlier entitled, Pimlico and Impenzi would sprawl over them, in the mornings and found some whole but not quite ripe, others with the tops eaten away. I did not want to think about what animal had done the damage. Carefully, I cut away that section, wrapped

Middle Passage. 'That was hundreds of years ago,' our guide said, surprised at her tears. I choked back my tears, but my heart was inundated.

At the wedding party, a young girl took to me. She kept wandering over to the table I shared with friends, to hold my hand and play with my earrings. The lady whom she went back to periodically watched us with a smile.

Late in the evening, when we the guests had flirted, danced, and eaten, the lady introduced herself as the child's mother. I surmised that she must be her adopted mother as their complexion shades could not have been more different.

It was not long before the mother wove me a story of her hardship and the help she needed with her daughter's education. She invited me to dinner. I went with my girlfriend from England. It was the first time I had seen the dramatic effect of skin bleaching. Her face and neck bore no resemblance to her arms and legs. It was as if a line had been drawn from the base of her neck to the top of her arm producing two entirely different people.

Looking back, I wished I had engaged her in conversation about it. At the time, I was mainly concentrating on fighting to conceal my puzzled – if not scornful – demeanour. As she told me her tale of woe, I thought that she should save the money she spent on skin bleach for her child's education.

Skin bleaching is one of those behaviours that defy understanding for me, especially being from a family where high self-image and positive self-concept came with the territory. In fact, tempering that self-love and self-belief was one of the biggest challenges that we had. Even in those days when, as new and strange minority in a new and strange country, we were sorely tested.

Ostensibly, people in Jamaica have supreme self-confidence, arguably bordering on arrogance. Yet there the remainder in foil, and left them all to ripen. They did so gloriously, and we feasted, gardener and friends who chanced by.

My mother called from Saint Catherine and asked about the pear tree, keen to taste that unusual variety.

I told her that it was unlikely she would get any as they were finishing fast.

We continued to compete with the dogs to get the pears. Sometimes we won, sometimes they did.

I think Pimlico and Impenzi knew they were not allowed to rub salt in our wounds by taking them through the house when they were the first to find them. But they still managed, when we were distracted, to rush through the house to the pool deck with their pear snack, where they ate with slow victorious delight. The health benefits were visible. They looked even more healthy than usual; shiny coats, limpid eyes, well-oiled joints.

One day I went to the tree and there was only one pear left hanging. I could not believe that we had eaten all but one in what seemed only a few days.

Fortuitously my mother visited that weekend. She was keen to know about the pear tree and bemoaned the fact that there was only one left. And more, that is was too high for us to pick. We shook the trees, even found a long stick, but alas, it did not have the required crooked end. The gardener would not be back until the Monday, so she accepted sadly that she would not get a taste of the pear this time round.

My mother packed to leave and decided to go one last time to the pear tree. There on the ground almost to order was the last pear of the season from our tree. It had the characteristic bite mark at the top but we did not care. Overjoyed, my mother cut off the tip and wrapped the rest in foil and took it home to ripen. Our beloved pear tree now stands bare of fruits.

We pay homage to her daily, longing for that time again. But we know there can never be a time like the first time when she so delighted us with the very first and the very last fruit from her virgin crop.

3 METAMORPHOSIS

One of my favourite short stories as a teenager was Metamorphosis by Franz Kafka. It is about a man who woke one morning to find he had transformed into a bug. I even like the word metamorphosis.

I often wonder whether metamorphosis will ever be embraced as an inevitable feature of life in Jamaica, or whether most people will continue to hang on to a world view that they were forced into, or that their forebears imbued in them hundreds of years ago.

A few years ago, I went to a friend's wedding in Gambia. It was my first time there and the country engaged all my senses.

My friend AM cried when we visited the island where slaves were kept before their ordeal through the

Middle Passage. 'That was hundreds of years ago,' our guide said, surprised at her tears. I choked back my tears, but my heart was inundated.

At the wedding party, a young girl took to me. She kept wandering over to the table I shared with friends, to hold my hand and play with my earrings. The lady whom she went back to periodically watched us with a smile.

Late in the evening, when we the guests had flirted, danced, and eaten, the lady introduced herself as the child's mother. I surmised that she must be her adopted mother as their complexion shades could not have been more different.

It was not long before the mother wove me a story of her hardship and the help she needed with her daughter's education. She invited me to dinner. I went with my girlfriend from England. It was the first time I had seen the dramatic effect of skin bleaching. Her face and neck bore no resemblance to her arms and legs. It was as if a line had been drawn from the base of her neck to the top of her arm producing two entirely different people.

Looking back, I wished I had engaged her in conversation about it. At the time, I was mainly concentrating on fighting to conceal my puzzled – if not scornful – demeanour. As she told me her tale of woe, I thought that she should save the money she spent on skin bleach for her child's education.

Skin bleaching is one of those behaviours that defy understanding for me, especially being from a family where high self-image and positive self-concept came with the territory. In fact, tempering that self-love and self-belief was one of the biggest challenges that we had. Even in those days when, as new and strange minority in a new and strange country, we were sorely tested.

Ostensibly, people in Jamaica have supreme self-confidence, arguably bordering on arrogance. Yet there are still many who despise themselves and others who conspire to encourage and perpetuate their self-loathing.

But not all by any means; I overheard some staff members taking with disdain and ridicule about bleachers. The staff members were the alluring mix of shades of complexion that constitute Jamaica.

'Dem no have no sense,' one said.

'If people no love me for me, dat's der pralem.'

'It's because dem can't read and write,' another said.

One of the other staff members felt it was the way they were brought up, the messages they got throughout their lives.

KL, a young woman who would clearly have made much of her life if born under different circumstances, was emphatic. 'I think they are stunted. My grandmother used to say if a plant does not get everything it needs to grow, its growth will be stunted.

They did not get everything. They need help,' she concluded.

They drew their supervisor JJ into the conversation. What did she think about the bleachers?

'To paraphrase Jude Judy,' she said, 'If they insist on being idiots, I can't help them.'

I joined the conversation and told them about something I had read in the news about a woman called Jennifer Teege. She is of dual heritage and discovered relatively late in her life that her grandfather was the notorious Nazi, Amon Goeth, knowledge that she has found difficult to deal with.

Teege believes, however, that her story is about the universal question of how to deal with the weight of the past in the present. She is clear that it is possible to gain personal liberation from the past. Interesting view, I said, as the past from which she needs liberation is only a couple of generations away.

'Importantly, I think Bob Marley is right,' KL said. 'It has to be a personal act of liberation. No one can cut your head open and set you free...'

4 COME-WE-STAY

I recently read an article about Kenya's policy to broaden the definition of marriage, and to include under that umbrella, unions that hitherto had not been considered legal.

One that caught my attention is a union called come-we-stay. The government's plan is to legitimise those lasting six months or more.

I Googled it and found that come-we-stay unions provoke a myriad of opinions about their advantages and disadvantages, especially for women and their resulting children.

As a young child in rural Saint Catherine in the early sixties, I remember two broad unions; marriage, where individuals were legally married, or cohabitation where individuals were called partners.

Years later, in that other country, it became fashionable among my liberal to the left-wing feminist circle of friends for couples to live together rather than marry, and the term 'partner' became oh-so-fashionable. Some couples, I think, even believed they had coined the term and invented the arrangement themselves. In fact, it was not at all fashionable to broadcast whether one was married or not. So all of us used the term 'partner' as a generic term for the man or woman we lived with or dated long-term.

Some of us who got married, to the opprobrium of many of our friends, even dispensed with the wedding ring and called ourselves Ms. Indeed, whether we were married or single, Ms was preferred to Miss or Mrs.

And why not? We argued. In those days, it was extremely unusual to see married men with wedding rings, and there was no distinction in titles for them to indicate whether they were married or not. So why should we as women be so branded? In further advancement of our position, most of us did not let go of our own surnames but appended the husband's name to it, giving us double-barrelled names. The more radical of us even completely refused to take on the husband's name, or to give the children of the union his surname.

None in my circle of friends considered it a status symbol to be married. Indeed, there were some friends whose marital status I did not know then, or now. The surnames they used were no help, nor were the surnames of their children or indeed whether the women wore wedding rings or not. It was never relevant, and marriage was most definitely not regarded as a badge of honour. Some of these unions endured, some did not. One wonders now how the statistics would stack. Did those legally married last longer than those who were not?

In those days, in my early- to mid-twenties, when I used to come to Jamaica on my annual holiday visits I was often asked the same question by men and women alike. 'Are you married?'

'No.'
'Are you a baby mother?'

'No.'

The looks of incredulity were both interesting and amusing to me.

It was in those years that I learnt of the concept of baby mother and understood that it defined one who is unmarried, and has a child or several children. In those years, I observed that the term was used exclusively for women from the poorer social class backgrounds, who may have children with one or more men, the baby fathers, and more often than not had started on this path of baby mothering as teenagers.

The baby fathers, by definition, seemed to be shadowy, mainly absent figures.

What are then the connections between partners in rural Saint Catherine in the 1960s, the middle-class liberals in that other country in the 1980s, come-we-stay unions in Kenya, and the baby mothers and baby fathers of contemporary Jamaica?

To my mind, the partners of 1960s rural Jamaica were, or aspired to be, a unit. Most often with grandparents in the same household, they worked, raised and supported their children together as a unit.

The middle-class liberals were educated and affluent individuals who made thoughtful choices that they could afford. Their choices did not generally disadvantage their children or the women. Their children were more often than not, like their parents, opportunities-enabled. They grew up immersed in diverse cultural and educational experiences, supported and guided by their parents until they too became independent achievers and useful contributing members of society.

And what of the come-we-stay unions and Kenyan's bid to legitimise them? Is there a connection between these come-we-stay unions, and the unions between baby mothers and baby fathers in Jamaica? It seems not. The unions between the baby mothers and baby fathers do not seem to last as long as six months, the period required to legitimise them.

.

5 BANK QUEUES

NE has the type of bank account that gives her the privilege of taking a ticket, sitting and waiting her turn, rather than standing in a queue to wait. It is the same privilege enjoyed by senior citizens, only better. She does not have to stand to be served; an overly comfortable seat is reserved for customers like her.

NE is a returnee, tiny in stature, but this is more than compensated for by her self-assurance and the confidence which an excellent education and supreme talent in the use of language give.

NE took her number, sat down, took out her electronic reader and waited for the 'dings' of the number machine. She waited patiently, slowly getting used to the inordinate waiting time that is customary in banks though still frustrated by it.

Two middle-aged men came in together, big and broad, as the local saying goes. In character, they drew everyone's attention with their loud talking and flowery gesticulating. They waved to the cashiers who waved back with beaming smiles. NE registered that they did not go over to the number machine. They stood by the seats, legs wide. The room resonated with the boom of their voices.

There was no 'ding' of the number machine but one of the men was waved over to her desk by the available cashier as her customer left. NE checked her number, checked the machine. That had not moved.

She thought, 'He must have been there before and went out for something.' Another period of time passed, another cashier became available; no movement from the ticket machine and the other man was waved forward by the cashier. NE approached the desk. 'I have a number, but neither of the last two people you served seemed to have one. What number are you serving?'

Before the cashier could speak, one of the men interrupted her with 'Expletive...expletive.... I don't need a ticket, and if I had a ticket, it would be number one.' Then, 'She tink she's in foreign now. You 'ave to wait, me a get serve now.'

The cashier kept her head down and continued serving him. The first man, not wanting to miss the opportunity for sport, joined in, 'Gal, shut up, si dung, and wait. Let de man do im business.'

The cashier laughed openly, enjoying her favourite customers' jibes.

Outnumbered and out of her depth, NE asked to see the manager. The manager responded feebly, 'You will be served next.' No explanation or apology.

That was not the end for NE. The letters she wrote went to managers local, national and regional. The branch manager who called with an apology was clearly perplexed. How could two individuals getting served before her cause such consternation?

Flouting queues in Jamaica is a national pastime.

It is commonplace to have people stretch over you to get served, or interrupt you to talk to a staff member. behaviour. Staff and customers collude in this behaviour.

Staff make excuses when you protest. 'He is only asking a question.' The answer to the question often takes minutes. Or, from the customer extending a long arm across your face to a staff member, 'Just do this for me nuh?'

Queue-jumping in banks is, however, not often as flagrant as in NE's case. It is usually subtle and fast.

An individual ignores the looping lines, heads to the front, puts a pile of something or other in front of the cashier, and disappears. The cashier takes it and puts it under the counter. She serves someone and then does not look up, let alone call the next in line.

She beavers away, serving customers who are not there.

These banking practices are immutable. The banks apparently believe that their customers have nothing better to do than to wait in their lines. I once spent seven hours in a bank opening a business account.

A section of NE's letter of complaint read, 'The hours I spent waiting in line in the bank, to be ignored by your staff who served her friends... could have been used to work at my business, and make revenue for this country, or do badly needed voluntary work in the community.'

6 A REASON TO LEARN

Recently a global education league table was published. Among other things, it concluded that the most significant factor in achieving a high ranking on the table was a culture that is supportive of learning.

I imagine that the first step to developing this prized culture of learning is to have a literate population, and second, for the population to have a thirst for knowledge.

It is staggering how many adults in Jamaica cannot read or write, belying the statistics of almost 90% literacy level. Everything seems to be in place to support learning. Education is free and compulsory, and there are adult schemes and programmes available all over the island.

So what are the barriers?

For a period of time, I ran adult literacy classes. When students came to learn, I was interested to hear why they felt they had not learnt to read so far. The reasons they gave were variations on a theme though none the less heart-wrenching. Parents wanted them to help in the fields. There was no money for fares, lunches, books, fees or uniform. Their parents couldn't read and could not help them, or did not consider schoolwork important. They were *bad* and were more out of the classroom than in. Teachers did not care if they learnt or not. They got confused with the letters, and their teachers thought they were dunces and did not try with them.

I was also interested in their reasons for coming back to school to learn.

There were the unsurprising ones of wanting to help their children, or even grandchildren, with their schoolwork. Likewise, wanting to learn before a new girlfriend or boyfriend found out that they could not. A few were getting anxious about disguising their illiteracy at work and wanted to learn before they were discovered.

There were also fascinating accounts from some men of expectant women abroad, from the USA,

Canada and the UK mainly, who had come to Jamaica on holiday, fallen in love with them, wanted to marry them and to move them abroad to live. These met-on-holiday boyfriends felt they needed to be able to read to travel. Some took lessons discreetly, keen to learn before that eagerly-anticipated date. Others were encouraged to do so and had their fees paid by their benefactor lovers from abroad.

A minority of students were quite enigmatic. They were invariably young men in their twenties, immaculately dressed in expensive designer gear and with supreme self-confidence. They either came to classes or were dropped off by friends who were likewise expensively dressed and drove impossibly expensive cars.

Interestingly, these students habitually brought state-of-the-art laptops to lessons and later, when these came on the market, tablet computers. The other signature accessories were the two smartphones that rested casually in leather holders on their slim hips. Whatever other purposes these computers served, the students enthusiastically learnt to download e-books and worksheets to practice their newly-acquired reading and writing skills away from class.

This young, enigmatic group was the most successful group of all. They were highly motivated, passionate in their eagerness to read and write. Each one tended to achieve his goal in a relatively short space of time, even if previously convinced that he was an incurable dunce.

The moral of the story seems to be that to develop a culture of reading, let alone a culture of education; students need to feel they have a reason for learning.

This seems elementary, but that is the stage where a lot of individuals seem to be here. As one student from the latter group commented shrewdly, 'I didn't have a reason to learn to read before.'

7 THEY CAN SWITCH ON YOU

A few years before I returned to live in Jamaica, I was on the North Coast on holiday. As usual, being in that part of the island, I hired a car.

Looking back, I am not sure what madness persuaded me to drive through the centre of downtown Montego Bay. At one point there were cars coming from every conceivable direction, none taking notice of road signs, each edging close to the other, no one stopping to look or give way and almost all seemed to be blowing their horns. In the melee were pedestrians, stepping off pavements and walking for metres in the centre or on the side of the road. Many, weaving in and out all unmindful of the tangle of moving cars around them.

Added to this were carts; four-wheel contraptions being pushed with a variety of wares; the soup man and his moving soup restaurant, the greengrocer with his colourful produce from the country, the ice and syrup man, the bread man, and more besides.

The cars were bad enough, but the pedestrians who threw me over the edge. They were on their phones, talking to companions, or more scarily seemingly in a trance, oblivious of the traffic.

At one point the confusion and the ruckus overwhelmed me. I took both hands off the steering wheel and shouted, 'I can't do this!' Everyone in the car laughed, easing the tension a little.

It may have been then, on another trip or when I had returned, that I heard stories of people attacking drivers even killing them, after accidents with pedestrians. The prevailing view is that if you collide with a pedestrian, regardless of the circumstances, the driver must be at fault. And if you are at fault you have to pay, there and then.

'So many people are walking incendiaries, and not just pedestrians,' was how BR, another returnee, explained it. She offered by way of explanation poverty, political frustrations, resentment, historical oppression, and hard lives. 'What is certain,' she said,

'is that people can explode on you at any given moment. What you see is not what you get. You have to be alert and aware in social interactions in this country.'

She told me that while she was in one of the tourist resorts on the North Coast, she and members of her family from abroad were at a craft street fair. They were walking leisurely past stalls with their attendant sellers. In true Jamaican style, the vendors were seducing them with their persuasive lyrics, pointing out things they were selling. Their sing-song voices and unmatchable patois made her smile.

Still in the ecstasy of being back after so many years away, she felt happy among them. She felt relaxed to be back at home, showing her family the different sights. She planned to get a standing carving or two; a colourful parrot on an extended pole had caught her attention, and perhaps a doctor bird.

They had parked, bought patties and soda, eating and drinking as they walked. They were too excited to sit and eat. Her family thought they might buy a few things too, to support the sellers. They needed nothing, so anything would do.

They responded lightly to the lyrics of the sellers, flirting with them too as the vendors tried to persuade them to buy this or that. They thought they would walk the whole length of the street, see what was on offer and then start again at the beginning. Her family warned BR to be modest. They knew how susceptible she was to the persuasive lyrics, so new, so expressive, so fresh, and so different from her former adoptive country. As they weaved in and out of the stalls, talking and laughing among themselves and with the sellers, something caught her grandson's eye. In rushing to it, he missed his step on the uneven pavement and dropped the bottle he was holding. It shattered. Before they had time to respond, they were confronted with a barrage of abuse and curses from the sellers who moments ago had jested with them.

'Unoo pick it up, unooou tink because unooou come from farign unooou can drop tings.' There were more curses and taunts, some of which they could not understand, some all too clear.

Confused and suddenly frightened at the sudden change of atmosphere, they hurriedly collected the pieces of the broken bottle, which they would not have dreamed of leaving anyway, and made hasty steps to their vehicles, and away from the area.

8 RETURNEES DEPORTEES

I was out volunteering one day when someone I had not met before joined the group. CP, whom I knew fairly well, introduced me. 'This is Vee, a returnee,' she said. Even as I was responding to the greeting, I was thinking, 'Why on earth would anyone introduce another person as a returnee? Why would anyone think that could in any way define me?

I complained to ND about it. She is a foreigner living in Jamaica. In her quiet, cynical way she pronounced, 'Don't you know that they regard returnees in the same way as they do deportees? It is as if they are saying, *you went away and should have stayed away. But now that you have been spewed back don't imagine that you can be one of us.*

I felt that was a bit harsh, until months later I was within earshot of a conversation where the subject of returnees came up. It seems to be on everyone's lips, I thought.

PG was originally from another Caribbean island. Although he is usually a man of few words, he is never afraid of controversy. 'Jamaica was glad about the migration of the poor and rural folk.' He spoke with authority. 'Jamaica did not have to be responsible for them, and it gave the country a bigger middle class.' He said as if only the middle class was useful to the island. 'As they were mainly country people they were not work-shy, and they were ambitious to better themselves too. They worked hard for themselves, and for Jamaica. Even from the outset, they sent money back to the grandparents to support the children. Ironically, though, that was the beginning of the remittance culture that some say is playing havoc with work ethics in Jamaica.

'What the country did not bargain for was that so many of them would return so many years later. In the beginning, people thought that if they came back at all, they would have done it after a few years when they had made a little something. When they had a few pounds in their pockets.

'No one thought they would have stayed so long and come back in the way they are doing now, well off, with their investment accounts and big pensions.' He paused. 'But there is a feeling in the country about that, about them, an undercurrent of feeling it seems to me. There is a definite feeling, and it is not always positive...'

We were interrupted and the conversation was left there. A few weeks later, I was out with ND, and MB, who is a well-travelled Jamaican but who has never lived abroad. We went to one of my favourite beaches, in an area favoured by returnees. The long white sandy beach was almost empty. There were only two other groups apart from us: young lovers frolicking in the water metres away, and a family with a large dog on a leash. Someone was frying chicken in one of the mansions facing the sea.

The spot we chose had no natural shade, but we had brought our beach umbrellas and quickly fixed them in place. Our dogs, Impenzi and Pimlico, having decided that the dog in the distance was no threat, were sprawled out in the sand under the cool shade of one of the umbrellas.

Later in the afternoon, after we had picnicked, swam, played around at the water's edge, walked and slept, I raised the subject of returnees. I told them what PG had said, and asked what they thought the feeling was that he talked about. ND, our resident cynic, said, 'That's easy; people resent and dislike them, both for going in the first place and for coming back. Even more than that, the country relegates them to a class of their own, the returnee.' Her tone was peppered with ridicule. 'It is not even a class,' she said, 'it is a kind of subset of outcasts.'

ND was convinced that the returnee is not fully integrated into society, that exclusion applies, either self-imposed or enforced by the locals. 'But there is the contradiction,' she said. 'The returnee is at the same time envied, resented, mocked, exploited, and ridiculed even as the country leeches onto them. Even as the locals grab what they bring back from their years of hardship and labour abroad.

'And yet the returnees foolishly keep coming with their open hearts, their open chequebooks, and their plentiful optimism,' she sneered.

MB interjected, 'That is the problem. They come with too much. Too much of everything. Too much cynicism of the old structures, too much scorn for the old beliefs and social hierarchies, too much self-love, too much love generally...too much money...and especially too much nostalgia....' She paused for effect.

'You know, folks can't stand people who have too much. People who are too much. Jamaicans don't like people who are *too much*; they say, *she too nuff, him too nuff.*

Life is tough for a lot of people here, so if you are *too nuff*, if you act like you are *too nuff*, you won't get on here.... You'll find it hard.'

ND felt that if there was a fault to be placed on the returnee, it was that they imagine they still share the same culture as Jamaicans who had not left. 'The culture they left died long ago; there is a new and a foreign culture to learn and to adjust to. They can't countenance that. And what is worse for them is that by the fact that they come *from foreign,* as everyone puts it, people think they are *too nuff.* So they are coveted, resented and hated. If they are tolerated, it is under sufferance. 'There is no winning for these returnees as far as I can see.'

9 CHICKEN

MN is an expat who originally came to Jamaica to be with her husband on a three-year contract. She is in her early twenties and had not previously travelled before coming to Jamaica.

Her confidence growing in her use of English, we were talking about food. 'Why do you only have ten dishes in Jamaica?' she asked me.

'Do we?' I responded, never having counted. I wasn't even sure she was saying what she wanted to say.

'And there are only five ways you cook chicken,' she persisted. 'In my country, there are hundreds of ways to cook chicken.' She wondered if I knew why, with such amazing, fresh ingredients and what she felt must be the richest soil in the world, Jamaicans are so afraid of experimenting with food.

'So chicken,' I said with a grin. She looked blank. Apparently humour is the last to come when learning a new language.

Food stories abound among the expats, if not among the returnees. ME is in Jamaica too on a contract. Unlike some of his compatriots, he came alone and without knowing anyone. Wishing to improve his English he avoids spending time socially with those who speak his mother tongue. He soon learnt too to distinguish between Jamaican patois and Jamaican Standard English, the latter the language of the educated middle class. He wanted to learn both, he said, and was doing especially well with patois.

ME sought friendship from colleagues in his company and behaved as he would in Europe, inviting them out to tea and to dinner.

'But no one ever invites me back,' he said, 'and when we go out, no one ever makes any effort to contribute to the bills. It is taken for granted that I will be paying, every time.'

'Not sure why that is,' I said, not wanting to tell him that had been my experience too when I first came back. The prevailing view is that if you have lived abroad if you look or speak differently to the general population, you must be rich, especially if you move in certain circles.

I have learnt now, I thought without saying. In his bid to build friendships, ME invited a colleague, JS, and his partner AG home to dinner. He asked the normal questions about what they liked to eat and what they did not eat. There were a few things they did not like so he, of course, excluded those from the list. JS said that he and AG loved pork, so ME decided on that. He thought he would also do some herb roasted sweet potatoes, and a mixed leaves green salad with avocados. Tons were falling from the tree in his garden. Dessert would be fresh local fruit. He knew his limitations in the kitchen.

The pork shoulder was seasoned with garlic, sage, thyme, basil, salt and pepper, olive oil and vinegar, which he said he had left overnight to marinate. It was still roasting on low heat when his two guests arrived.

His colleague's partner, AG, commented on the wonderful smell. 'I've been saving myself,' she said smiling.

JS asked, 'What type of pork is it, brown stew or jerk?'

Confused, ME said, 'Neither. I am cooking a dish from my country.'

'Oh, I only eat jerk pork or brown stew pork,' he said.

'You'll like it.' AG said persuasively. 'It smells lovely, and looks delicious,' she said licking her lips as ME opened the oven to show them the now perfectly roasted pork.

When it was time to eat, JS would not eat the pork. 'I know I won't like it,' he insisted, 'and I've never had sweet potatoes like that. I don't like those bits on it.'

'It is just herbs, salt and pepper,' ME coaxed.

If AG was embarrassed, she didn't show it. She ate, only pausing periodically to voice praise. Once or twice she said, referring to her partner, 'He's like that,' and told stories of times when they had gone out and he hadn't eaten because something 'turned him off.'

ME was mortified but after a while ceased trying to coax him, and resisted the temptation to suggest sending out to one of the local jerk centres. There were two famed outlets within ten minutes' drive.

ME told me that the incident had occurred soon after he came to the island. He had never invited anyone else back again, he said and puts his twenty pounds weight gain down to that. I was puzzled.

'I'm not used to eating dinner alone,' he said. 'So I eat out; jerk, brown stew, curry, baked chicken, or jerk pork and fried fish with fried plantain, festival, rice and peas or plain rice...

I wondered if those were NE's ten dishes.

10 THE GARDEN

They had contracted the landscape designer, HH, whom the architect had recommended. She had a string of qualifications and had come with an equal amount of verbal endorsements. Those were the days before they understood that such recommendations meant little.

HH's design was amazing, and viewed in the chilly grey drizzle of that other country the designs looked especially glorious. It was hard to visualise that the rocky acre of land with the unforgiving elevation and out-of-control trees and bushes could be transformed as HH conceived. They could hardly wait.

It did not cross their minds that they would use anyone but HH. Her vision had completely seduced them. She had to be retained until the patch of land had been transformed into a garden as she saw it.

Now, installed in their apartment to await the completion of the house, the garden was next. HH, having been paid for the drawings, could now turn her attention to sourcing and planting, and to installing the sprinkler system and footpaths. They asked her to price everything and let them know.

As the house went up, it had slowly dawned on them that there were a returnee price and a Jamaican price for everything. Initially, she had dismissed what her sister, a nine-year returnee, had said to her, 'Don't keep converting everything back into pounds and saying it is cheap. It is not. They are ripping you off.'

They had not listened to her sister when they chose the Quantity Surveyor or the Contractor. 'They belong to the professional associations,' she had said as if that eased every anxiety. But as the house went up, and the variations and increases in prices came almost weekly, she wished they had listened.

Having learned, they now listened and obtained one other quotation for the garden. JF's quotation was fifty percent cheaper than HH's, but he said immediately that he was not a landscape designer. 'I have never been to school for it but I know the land. And I know and understand plants and flowers.' He had a farm too, a few hundred acres that he was leasing from a local landowner. He planted organic vegetables for local hotels, he said.

They liked his matter of fact way of speaking, his unapologetic description of what he could and could not do.

He would not be able to put anything on paper, he said. 'I carry it all in my head. I can see it clearly in my mind. I look at the land and it comes to me. All the plants and where I am to put them come to me.'

They asked him to take a look at HH's design. He paused for ages at the terracotta pots, and even longer at the water features. He read aloud names of plants that they had never heard of, herbage that had twisted their tongues when they had tried to pronounce them.

They thought he would never speak. The man he had brought with him, whom he introduced as one of his planter men, went with him as they wandered the land. They trotted behind both of them, the sound of construction still heavy in the air.

Finally, JF spoke, 'Most of these plants that she put on here won't grow on this land,' he said, tapping the paper. 'Not the right soil for them. Yes, she will source them and plant them but they will never thrive. She'll be wasting your money. And water features and terracotta pots are not things I deal with,' he said decisively.

Since they had returned and the construction had started, a sinking feeling had become part of their everyday experience. The excitement and elation of leaving that other country and building a house in the land they called home, despite leaving when they were children over forty years ago, were fast seeping away. Half the time they felt spent, overwhelmed, and afraid.

'Are you sure?' she said.

'Yes. I know the soil up here.'

All that money wasted, he thought. When will it end? She thought.

True to his word, JF started the work a week later. They watched him supervise the unloading of trucks full of topsoil, equipment for the irrigation system and footpaths, plants galore; shrubs, palms, fruit trees and ground cover plants.

They watched him instruct his group of men what to put where what to plant first and what to do next.

She was nervous that the big-booted builders would damage the delicate saplings until she saw how careful the planters were to direct them where they could and could not walk. 'We are not romping,' she heard one telling a builder who tried to ridicule his tenderness toward the plants. 'Dem no young babies,' he had said with derision.

'Me sey me naay romp, so no come near me plants!' He was not smiling. The message got through.

They wandered around with the planters sometimes. She particularly liked the oldest man, whom her friend's six-year-old son called the two-hundred-year-old planter man. 'You are going to have the best garden up here,' he said as he carefully removed a bougainvillea sapling from a small black bag and placed it gently in one of the holes he had dug. 'And the hibiscus you have all over the place will bring hummingbirds of all descriptions, and this plant,' he pointed to a fine-leafed plant that she did not recognise, 'will turn white every Christmas-time. And this bougainvillea fence will be the prettiest fence you have ever seen.' She tried but could not imagine it.

One side of the property had a concrete fence that had been rendered and painted. They now decided that had been a mistake, and refused to waste any more money on that type of fencing. Instead, they installed a wire fence on which they hoped the bougainvillea would spread. It would be an exercise in deferred gratification, they knew.

One of their neighbours, on seeing the wire fence beside which the bougainvillea was planted, had tried to embarrass her in a Residents' Association meeting.

'Your house is stunning but that wire fence is totally awful, looks totally awful. It's not becoming to the area,' he had blurted in his American drawl. She had ignored him, looking forward to the time when He would eat his words. That time was delayed when heavy rains came and washed away all but a few of the new saplings. The planting had been finished by then. She recalled JF. 'I'll set some more. And you must tell your neighbour to take care of his drain is him cause them to wash away.' She took pictures every three months or so, hardly noticing that a transformation was occurring before her very eyes.

The house finished, they had the house-warming; scores of friends came from that other country to celebrate with them.

The dry weather came, then the rains; a few hurricanes threatened but passed by. One or two tropical storms came but did little or no damage. Their garden flourished steadily. The two trees that had been left standing after the land had been cleared, the ackee and mango, bore abundantly.

A few years passed without harvesting anything from those JF had planted, then one or two began to bear fruit; sweetsops, grapefruits, plantains, bananas, avocados, June plums, guavas....They enjoyed and shared their bounty with pride, amazement and joy.

New flowers bloomed too, showing off their extraordinary shapes and colours while their fragrances filled the air.

As the old planter man had said, several varieties of hummingbirds made the garden their haunt. They had never imagined that there were so many varieties of hummingbirds. It seemed every conceivable bird known in the Caribbean passed through, endless varieties of butterflies darted in and out of flowers while crickets a-plenty competed with the constant music of the songbirds.

Tiny creatures that flew, crawled and hovered in and out of the plants fascinated them. Audacious mongoose startled them at times. The nightly fireflies made them smile. And they stood in awe at the odd bird of prey that passed by, lingering for moments on the towering queen palm tree in a neighbouring property.

Occasionally now they allowed contentment. That had been long in coming.

One day she came across some old photographs of the newly-planted garden on her computer. Six years had passed and they lived surrounded by glorious mature flowers, herbs, shrubs and fruit trees of almost every description.

Each season there was something to reap. The two Christmas flowering trees, firmly rooted either side of their huge vehicular and pedestrian iron gates, turned white in early December and sometimes lasted until early February. Each year she planned to find out its name.

The bougainvillea had spread as she had dreamed. The gardener fought to keep it under control. Her doubting neighbour, long driven away by the unforgiving economic downturn, was not around to eat his words.

Passers-by and visitors alike often stand in admiration. The ugly wire fence, beautifully hidden, supports a tangle of blazing pink, red and white bougainvillea extending from the front to the back of the garden.

At the end of the seventh year, they invited the gardener and his team back for lunch-time Christmas drinks and food. The two-hundred-year-old planter man was still going strong. They had music, and he danced with energy to mento and ska, his tall, slender frame twisting and dipping like a young man's, in moves that they had only ever seen in old-time films.

Before he left, he toured what he called his garden. They looked up in unison as a formation of egrets flew low directly over their heads, their white bellies and graceful flapping wings as clear as the day. 'Can there be a more magical sight?' the two-hundred-year-old planter man said, his eyes following them towards the Caribbean Sea in the distance, and out of sight.

'Wow!' she exclaimed.

They wandered around slowly for some time. He did not speak but studied and carefully examined the fruits of his handiwork.

Now and again, a faint smile brushed his lips, and hers too.

11 URINATING IN PUBLIC

Men urinating in public are a common sight in Jamaica. Men of all ages clearly do not think it unacceptable in any way to stop by the side of the road and urinate in full view, and with uncaring abandon.

True, public toilets are not readily available, but restaurants and petrol stations are extremely relaxed about individuals using their facilities.

Perhaps we should excuse these men. No doubt they have medical conditions. But do so many men have medical conditions that they cannot wait for the next restaurant or petrol station, or until they get home to urinate? I think not.

It just seems to be an acceptable part of the culture for grown men to pee in public. Notions of self-respect, respect for others, manners, hygiene (for where do these men wash their hands afterwards?) and awareness of how this might be viewed by others do not seem to form any part of their thinking.

There was recently an interesting article on this subject of urinating in public on the BBC website. It seems that it is also prevalent in India. Some disgusted individuals there have tried to shame men into breaking this habit. In one State, volunteers attempted to do this by drumming and blowing whistles when they caught anyone urinating in public.

Our method here could be the car horn, I thought. Car horn blowing is used in Jamaica to communicate a range of emotions, instructions and messages. I am not sure whether it has been used to express outrage at men urinating in public. After reading the article about India, I decided to blow the horn the next time I saw a culprit. As it turned out, it was the very next time I went out in my car. Unfortunately for me, the man in question thought I must be someone he knew.

On hearing the blast of my horn, he spun round while still performing the dastardly act, member in one hand as he waved enthusiastically with the other. That being much more than I had bargained for, I decided never to try that again.

It may well be that we have lost the battle with this generation of men. It is too much part of their culture, if not the culture of the island. These men clearly do not consider the extremely rare possibility of being taken to court and fined; they ignore public service announcements and are bereft, it seems, of morals when it comes to this area of their lives.

It seems that parents need instead to focus on their children, to inculcate in them behaviours that we consider acceptable as a society, and discourage behaviours that we consider socially unacceptable.

Grown men urinating in public should undoubtedly be on the second list.

12 THIS THING ABOUT RESPECT

There is an almost clinical obsession with the concept of respect in Jamaica.

It is one of those words that have water-like fluidity, meaning different things to different people, but always suggestive of power struggles and angst.

More often than not it seems to have the capacity to take on a life of its own.

There are countless stories about individuals who consider they have been disrespected resorting to violence, and perhaps more frequently, walking out of their jobs. There is scarcely a person or business, it seems, that has not had the term thrown at them when a member of staff has walked away from a job.

Poca is not dissimilar to any other labourer in Jamaica. His complexion is weather-beaten and he has a lean and solid frame; the type of frame that many models and film stars would spend a fortune on gyms and personal trainers to acquire.

His frame is not the result of dedicated sessions at the gym, however, but born of consistent hard work as a gardener for three families; one day here, two days each here and there.

What is most striking about Poca is his mild, compliant manner and his knowledge about the medicinal properties of herbs and plants around the garden. If a member of the family breathes that he/she is suffering from a condition, he soon appears in the kitchen with a bundle of herbs to soak and drink, boil and drink, or infuse in a bath.

Poca speaks in dense riddles, making conversation with him both challenging and interesting. However, although one may not be able to decipher everything he says, one always catches a few sentences of undeniable wisdom, gems gleaned from experience working hand in hand with nature.

Poca is always effusive in his appreciation when given gifts. On pay days in particular, when he receives his wages he recites with earnest, 'Respect. Thank you.' All while maintaining steady eye contact, which in itself is unusual. It is quite common to receive an 'OK' when the response should be, 'thank you.' Not so Poca; he is never short on manners.

On receiving his Christmas hamper and monetary bonus, his lyrics are almost poetic. 'Respect. Much respect. You are a true lady. Thank you. Respect,' he recited, his palm resting over his heart.

On his return to work after the Christmas period, he was overheard to say he had walked out of one of his two-days-a-week job because he was not being respected. I did not hear what his employer had, or had not done.

It may be that preoccupation with being accorded respect is due to a range of historical, societal and

73

cultural factors. Indeed, it seems to be linked in no small way to the self-image of those preoccupied with it. What is clear, however, is that Jamaicans are extremely sensitive about being disrespected. Being slighted in any way, intentional or unintentional, is clearly viewed as a cardinal sin. It seems that workers, in particular, would sacrifice job security and regular pay to make that point and assert their right to be respected.

Poca was clearly agitated and wanted to talk. I was interested because his employer had recommended him to us. Even more, he complains continually about being short of money. 'A know the pay me get is better dan what most people get, but di money still done in bills even before me get it...' is his usual complaint. I asked him why he had walked out on his employer when the job was secure, and he needed the money. I suggested that the best course of action would have been to talk to his employer about his grievance, or, at least, waited until he had found another job before leaving. He was adamant that he had been disrespected, and no amount of talking would make amends. 'I can't work for anyone who no respect me,' he insisted.

Even while wondering whether he did indeed have good cause, I felt the seeds of nagging unease. How long will it be, I wondered before we unwittingly do something deemed disrespectful by him?

13 NIGHT SKIES

As a young child in the glorious hills of Saint Catherine, light pollution was not a concept we had heard of. Our world knew nothing of pollution, light or otherwise. As children, our night skies were part of our lives that we defined in simple terms. We had starry nights, moonlit nights or just dark nights. The wonder of the galaxy was a fact of life, like the hills around us and the lights of Kingston in the distance below.

In the same way, our relationship to the night skies was straightforward; dark nights were to be feared because the duppy (ghost) stories took on, even more, sinister forms. Moonlit nights enabled later bedtimes, and so more time to play. And both dark nights and moonlit nights gave us skies packed full of stars; twinkling, shooting, bright ones and dim ones. Yet danger lurked in them, we grew up believing; count them, but stop at 99. Get to 100 and you'll drop down dead.

Bob Mizon of Campaign for Dark Skies stated that,

'Many children growing up today will never see the Milky Way; never see the unimaginable glory of billions of visible stars shining above them.'

Indeed, in one part of that other country there is an area which is given special night skies protected status because it is feared that light pollution is slowly seeping its way into the country, and if nothing is done, night skies will be no more.

Back home in Jamaica, it took me a while to get in the habit of looking up again after nearly four decades of having nothing to look up for.

A member of my family is positively enthralled by night skies and calls me outside regularly to look up. While we gaze upwards in wonder, she reminds me of the lessons I learnt years and years before in school; that as well as the extraordinary beauty and wonder, we are actually watching stars that vary in ages from a few million to several billion years old. This is because, she reminds me, their lights take hundreds of thousands of years to get to us. This means that every time we look up, we are looking back in time. How amazing is that?

Thankfully, we still have many areas of Jamaica where night skies can be seen in all their glorious wonder. If you are lucky enough to be in one of these areas, here or indeed elsewhere in the world, it's worth looking up now and again. Maybe you will find yourself in awe.

14 PITYABOUT THE PEOPLE

NK is in her mid-twenties. She was not born in

Jamaica, nor were her parents, but her grandparents

were. Both sets of grandparents had lived in that other

country and had returned before NK was born.

Her parents wanted her to know her grandparents

well, so took her, or sent her, to Jamaica to be with

them every summer from the time she was eighteen

months old. NK continued going when she was at

university. Spending every summer with her adoring

grandparents on both sides gave her enduring love for

Jamaica. For years, she saw the island through the

seductive cloud of white sand beaches, so-called high-

end communities, exclusive villas and hotels, and road

trips to parishes and towns that engaged all her

senses. She was vocal about her love, identifying with Jamaica, she said, more than with that other country.

Her parents got used to hearing that, but were surprised when she decided to move to the island after leaving university, eventually to start a business, she said. Though they were taken aback, even disappointed, they tried hard not to show it. She had always been fiercely independent. Own way, as the Jamaicans would say.

They helped her to purchase an apartment on the North Coast, waved her off at the airport and waited, for what they were not sure.

Her maternal grandmother, BK, told them, 'Don't worry about her, she'll come and have a long holiday and then go back to her nice prospects in London...'

In Jamaica, none of her grandparents' friends, all of them returnees, were enamoured by the idea of this young girl coming to live in Jamaica. Their emphasis was always on the young.

Her paternal grandmother, AL, said, 'Jamaica is not for young people. There is nothing here for you. Only us old people with our nostalgia should come back.'

Her grandfather, AE, reminded his wife, 'She is not coming back. She is not a returnee like us. She has migrated. You ever dreamed of that? She is doing in reverse what we were forced to do when we went over there in the 50s.' He laughed long and hard. Finally catching his breath, he said, 'I am delighted though that my favourite grand-daughter is only a drive away – for the time being, at least...' he concluded with a smirk.

BK invited her to visit for the weekend. They lived at different ends of the island so NK was glad for the opportunity. She hoped they would invite some young people. She had joined one or two voluntary organisations and was getting to know a few people. But developing new friendships was harder than she had imagined it would be. She had so little in common with most of them; not education, not travel, not experience, not outlook, not culture. Early days, though, she thought.

NK arrived at her grandparents' to find an elderly couple, the Browns, there for the weekend too. They were returnees whom her grandparents had met on one of their Returnee Association's day trips.

The Browns had married in Jamaica in the fifties and had gone to that other country soon after. She trained and worked as a nurse, and he worked for the transport service. They had been back a few years now, they informed her, and had bought, not built, a house. 'We heard about the stress of that. We weren't prepared to go through that at our age.' Savings, pensions and children born and living in that other country secured their future.

The Browns went back to England every year for at least a month, they said. They did so to spend time with the grandchildren. They stayed longer if they were needed by one of the children to look after a new baby for the mother to return to work, or as happened recently, when one of their daughters was having major surgery.

Their lives in Jamaica were full, it seemed; they had their Church, their residents' and returnee associations, all providing them opportunities to meet new people. 'And to go around the island,' Mrs. Brown said. 'We have at least two trips each month, one with each association. And the church always has events.'

Mr Brown had his garden too. He delighted in it and boasted about what he was growing and how much he was able to give away each season.

The Browns were definitely contented to be back home in Jamaica so NK was puzzled by their scepticism of her decision.

They were eating lunch on the infinity pool deck, Kingston spread below them in the distance. It was a clear day, and she could pick out various landmarks in New Kingston. The John Crow and the Blue Mountains provided the backdrop.

'Jamaica is beautiful. No one can deny that,' BK said. 'Pity about the people.'

NK took immediate offence. How could anyone say something like that, about a whole group of people? She said as much.

Her grandfather agreed with BK. 'My dear, you will see. There are some good people, of course, but they cower away behind their security grilled houses, locked inside their air-conditioned, heavily-tinted vehicles. You don't see or hear them much.'

'The people like yourself, from your own class background,' his wife said, 'understand the society. They don't mix with any and everybody. I think they are all frightened.'

"What are they frightened of?' NK asked. 'The gun crimes are mainly well away from where they would live, or go.'

BK did not give her a direct answer. Instead, she told NK, 'When I came here first, I was quick to invite people I met to dinner at the house. No one from here ever invited me back.'

'Why not?' NK asked.

'Not really certain. You can't ask them,' Mrs Brown said. 'You can only guess that they are wary of letting people they haven't known for years into their lives.'

'They keep everyone out, the good and the bad. Even the good soon turn bad out here,' her husband said.

'And you have to protect yourself since everyone thinks you are rich. You don't know them from Adam but they want you to give them things. And once you help, they fasten onto you. Will even hurt you if you don't continue giving...'

'Well, the ordinary people will. The ones you would use as your helper and gardener. They are the ones who always have their hands open. They have their plenty children and their hard luck stories.'

Their two helpers cleared away the main course and brought ice cream and fruit salad for desserts.

Stories continued about those they described as foolish returnees, 'They come and throw everything wide open. They show off all the time, giving over-large tips to the boys who carry their groceries to their car, talking loudly in supermarkets about what they have and don't have. Advertising the fact that they come from foreign. I see them, inviting every little builder man, this and that little person they hardly know into their lives. Next thing you hear, they rob them or even kill them...'

'And you can't get a husband out here, you know...' Mrs Brown said with a wink.

'Gosh!' NK exclaimed at the sudden change of subject. She wondered whether that was why they thought she was in Jamaica. She had heard of many girls from abroad who came hunting for the men they thought were in short supply in that other county.

'...Not from the ordinary ones, anyway. Not from the little people.'

NK was beginning to find the discussion intolerable. She was being lectured. Did her parents put her grandparents up for this? They did not always say what they thought to her face, but she knew them.

'I would say, she could find a partner here if she looked in the right places, but most of the men here are definitely not in her league. They are not at the same stage as the men you will find over there. Over where you were born. Where you come from,' she emphasised. 'Most of the men here are not at the same stage in their thinking about women and relationships. Some in Kingston and at the universities, maybe. But it will be hard to find them.'

The conversation continued along those lines for the entire weekend. She could see that her grandparents and their friends were happy living in

Jamaica and would not consider going back. Why was it not good for her too?

As the weekend wore on she tried once or twice to shift the conversation to more positive things, filled as she was with the intense joy that still enveloped her about her new life.

Not able to change their conversation she let them talk, enjoying her grandparents' home, the food and the sun. It is because they are old. That's why they are so negative. I am young. It will be different for me. My experiences will be totally different.

15 FAST DRIVING

There is a saying that the only thing people do fast in Jamaica is to drive.

Both men and women boast about how fast they drive. For instance, one frequently hears stories of the impossibly short time they claim it takes them to get from, say, Kingston to Montego Bay. One of them even insisted, 'I can only control my car when I am driving fast.'

There are some interesting questions around this whole issue of driving on the island. My first experience of this was many years ago on one of our annual vacation trips. I was an experienced driver of many years in that other country but had suddenly become nervous about driving in Jamaica. This was odd as I had driven on all my previous trips when we had borrowed either my father's eleven-seater Land Rover or my mother's Mini-like 4-seater Toyota, and wagered that we could touch every parish in a day. I think we managed it once or twice, sharing the driving, leaving at the crack of dawn and returning very late at night.

Then I saw a dramatic accident, which had the usual ingredients of unbelievable madness; too-fast driving, overtaking around a blind bend, on road conditions that in no way permitted it. So we took to hiring cars with drivers, insisting that the cars had to have seat belts (another inexplicable fact is that many people take the seat belts out of their cars), with strict instructions that the driver could not drive too fast.

One of our drivers, after a week or so of getting to know us and driving as we asked, relaxed a bit, even perhaps forgetting the professional line he was supposed to take. When asked where he had taken his test, replied he had never taken a test because he knew someone at one of the offices, and he had bought his licence from him. He had a glimmer in his eyes when he said that, so we hoped he was joking.

One cannot help but wonder, though. Could it be possible that there are drivers out there who did not take driving lessons, let alone a driving test? The ones who habitually ignore the speed limit. Those who overtake across solid white lines, around bends, or over the brows of hills. Those who pull out into the line of oncoming vehicles without seeming to look. Those who habitually force drivers off the road and drive like bats out of hell on the wrong side of the road. The ones who overtake several cars simultaneously, uncaring of the line of traffic hurtling towards them, and the ones who have no concept of stopping distances.

A friend told me that when she went for her test, even though she had been driving for years in that other country, had a clean licence and was a double graduate, she was asked to read several simple passages a number of times. Not the one paragraph or so stipulated, but several. Then, when she had successfully completed the manoeuvres required for the test, she was told she had failed because she had not made a hand signal to turn right. Nonplussed, she related this story to friends. 'He wanted you to pay him,' was the most common response, said in a tone of how did you not know that? Indeed, some were surprised that she had bothered to go for the test at all, asking whether she did not know anyone who could have got the licence for her. Others quoted the varying fees that different testing officers would accept to give you a licence without having to bother with the test. Again, one can never be sure whether these are anecdotal, urban myths or indeed rural myths, but one wonders.

One wonders, too, where is the ability to generalise in Jamaican drivers? Do they never learn from the mistakes of others? Do they ever see the annual statistics of road fatalities?

Usually, you see an accident and, for a short period of time, at least, you check your speed, you observe the road conditions more carefully and you watch the distance between your car and the one in front. You think, I don't want to die on the road, or I don't want to be lying in a ditch unconscious waiting for the emergency services.

Apparently there is no such internal dialogue, or worse, no checks on behaviour as a result of past or recent experiences on the road.

One comes across this scene, painfully familiar to anyone who drives on the island. It can happen without warning. It is a beautiful sunny day, with almost cloudless blue skies. You are cruising in your vehicle, the Caribbean Sea on your left, the Cockpit Mountains with their blue-green shimmer adding drama to your right. The roads are dry, there are no potholes. You are, after all, on the smooth, newly-completed North Coast Highway. It is just another glorious day in paradise.

Suddenly there is a build-up of traffic and you have to come to a stop. You are stuck behind this line of traffic for minutes. In front individuals fling open their car doors, leaving them wide open as they saunter along the road, the pavement or the grass verge. You wait. Some, finally return to their cars and pull over; others, having had their eyes full, drive away.

Eventually, you are able to proceed and you arrive at the scene of interest, a familiar sight. There is a wrecked car in a ditch. You are told by those in your car that there are several people trapped inside, or in some cases dazed outside.

One or two are prone and seemingly lifeless. Another vehicle is across the central reservation in a position that defies logic. You drive on shaking your head, or saying knowingly, 'Someone was speeding.'

The intelligent drivers slow down and observe the speed limit, reflecting how those lying dead or injured may well have been them.

Suddenly, you see in your wing mirror a line of traffic overtaking three or four cars at high speed, each within a hair's breadth of the others' bumpers. No doubt among them are the same drivers whom we left gawking at the earlier accident. You hold your position because any second one of those in the line overtaking will suddenly veer to your left onto the hard shoulder, passing on the inside, or one will cut in sharply in front of you, just before colliding with the oncoming vehicles, and missing your car by centimetres. Several cars on the correct side of the road swing to the hard shoulder to avoid colliding with those overtaking. The Kamikaze drivers disappear into the distance.

A little way along you see cars flashing their headlights warning you that there are police with their speed guns ahead. You pray that at least one of those on their suicide mission has been caught. You get to the spot and find that the police are alone. The Kamikaze drivers are attuned to these altruistic warning flashing lights and, as usual, manage to slow down in time until they have passed the police speed traps. Or until they are finally and completely stopped by another driver like them, on their daily gamble with death.

Often it seems, however, it is not these drivers who are finally and completely stopped. It is that child in a minibus or taxi going to school, doing the normal schoolchild things, who has not yet even learnt to drive. It is that child who is thrown from the vehicle and whom the papers later lament is pronounced dead at the scene, as the drivers escape back on the road sustaining only minor injuries.

16 ONE MORE THING ABOUT FAST DRIVING

To borrow a little from Bob Marley, *there is so much things to say,* on this issue of driving in Jamaica. Just one more thing from me, though. Someone I know well – let's call her Anna – had an accident nearly four years ago.

It was a two-lane road in a built-up area in the tourist hub of the island. By his own admission, the driver – let's call him Dane – had been stuck behind a line of vehicles. There were no cars on the other side, so he took the chance to overtake, or 'pass' as the policewoman who was his supporting witness said in court.

He had been driving on the wrong side of the road for a good 100 metres when cars started to appear on that side. In his haste to get onto the correct side, he saw a gap, swung in, lost control of his vehicle and collided with Anna's car that was stationary waiting on a side road. Due, no doubt, to his speed, he careered onto the pavement and crashed into a tree.

One of his two female passengers was unconscious at the scene, with the other trapped in the vehicle. The emergency services were called. It was feared that the unconscious woman would die. Fortunately, she did not, although all sustained serious injuries.

Several witnesses, including the driver who had left the gap at the intersection, as he too waited in the traffic jam, gave similar accounts of a speeding van driver on the wrong side of the road swinging in and crashing into a stationary car.

Anna was not physically injured but was completely traumatised. She did not drive for months. After the accident, she duly went to the police station, gave her statement, and provided the names and telephone numbers of several individuals who had witnessed the crash. Incidentally, Jamaicans are at their most altruistic at the scene of an accident. A complete stranger had stayed with Anna until the police came; he had driven her to the hospital, called her partner and waited with her until he arrived.

Police accident investigators apparently made inquiries for their report. To cover all bases, Anna took what turned out to be very good advice and secured the services of a reputable, independent team of accident investigators. They made their reports too.

Anna waited to hear when she would be called to be a witness for the State, as she had been told by the police that the driver was being prosecuted for, among other things, dangerous driving. He had, after all, driven across an unbroken white line, well above the speed limit on the wrong side of the road.

The resulting account of the comings and goings of the police, the court system and the insurance company (that is another story) is stranger than fiction.

One day, out of the blue, Anna received a call from one of the traffic police officers who had arrived at the scene. The woman police constable (WPC) asked Anna to meet her in a car park near the police station. This, of course, struck her as odd, but Anna, a returnee and new to the island, decided that perhaps the officer was busy and wanted to hand her the very delayed accident report en route to somewhere else. Anna asked a friend to accompany her. The friend, a local, was suspicious and for the entire forty-five minutes that they waited, making several calls to the officer to enquire where she was and why they had to meet in a car park bent Anna's ear with her view that something untoward was going on.

Not persuaded but irritated by having to wait in a hot car for almost an hour, Anna went into the police station and asked to speak with the Superintendent to whom she related the story. The Superintendent thought Anna must have misunderstood the officer. No police officer would ask anyone to meet them in a car park. After all, the file for the accident was stored at the station.

Anna left the police station perplexed and went back to wait for news of the police accident reports, and for the case to be called. About a week later she received another call from the same WPC, informing her that Anna, not the other driver, was being charged with causing the accident.

There followed four years of court appearances; unwritten, incomplete, mislaid, lost then recovered accident reports, sandwiched between blatant lies and half-truths from Dane and the WPC of car park fame.

The latter was never an eye-witness to the accident, and came to immortalise the phrase, he was not overtaking a line of traffic across a solid white line because that would be an offence; he was just passing them.

The astute, long-suffering judges (because it ran into several different judges over the four years and twenty-seven court appearances) did a site visit with

Anna, the traffic police officers and Dane, whose account of the accident changed almost daily. When

Anna was finally exonerated, the judge summarised that Dane had given five different versions of the accident.

Anna was never able, nor did she try, to prove what her attorney suspected: that Dane knew the officer. It was certainly strange that often during the

WPC's statement and cross-examination in court,

She slipped up several times and called him by his first name.

More profoundly, Anna was never able to establish whether the WPC was indeed a corrupt officer who made the decision of prosecution based on payment received, or not received. And there were countless other questions, among them: who is accountable for the flagrant waste of taxpayers' money? Who notices?

Who does anything about it, and about officers like the WPC?

Certainly those who knew about the case insisted that it was highly irregular for only one of the drivers in such an accident to be prosecuted, or for a case to begin with no written accident report, as that case did.

My friend tells me that one of her enduring memories of those four years of court appearances was the constant surprise of her fellow-accused, who waited in the long, hot, battered hall for their names to be called into Court One, Two, Three or Four... 'Whey you doing here?' They would ask, looking her up and down.

At first, she answered simply, 'Traffic.' The questioners always retained the perplexed expression, leaving Anna wondering whether she had misunderstood that too, as she had been told she had misunderstood the WPC's invitation to meet her in a car park. After being asked it once too often for her fragile temper, she took the next questioner on, 'I said traffic. Don't you understand that? Traffic accident.'

The unfortunate man examined her carefully, taking in her linen-suited, carefully groomed appearance, and polished standard English. 'So why you never just pay de officer dem? You fool or what? The likes of you always just pay dem aff. Dem never come to court. Me never see one of you in court before.

If me had de money, me would pey dem alf meself. Who would come to dis ya place if him ave de chance to pey dem?'

17 INVENTIONS AND REINVENTIONS

There is an anecdote among returnees that if you wish to reinvent yourself, you need to migrate and return after a few years to your country of origin.

It seems there is more than a little truth in this.

Recently I invited someone to a voluntary club meeting. She is a returnee, a retired nurse now enjoying a life straddling two cultures. As we walked up the path to the meeting room, she stopped abruptly and asked, 'By the way, does someone called CJ come to your meetings?' I told her I did not know anyone by that name. She breathed an obvious sigh of relief.

She proceeded to tell me that she knew CJ in that other country. In fact, she knew him quite well, as he was married to one of her relatives. CJ had been a taxi driver for many years when he was put forward to be a

JP by a community group. Living in Jamaica now, he shamelessly masquerades as a retired judge from that other country. Indeed, even his wife calls him *Judge* when they are in company.

Then there is the young woman, born and bred in that other country, a progeny of those who had migrated in the rush to make a better life. She was an optometrist over there, where one is required to have a first degree but not necessarily a doctorate. After being here for a few weeks, no Ph.D. in sight, she started calling herself Doctor, even including it on her business cards.

Even though puzzling, it may well be said that the former is innocuous. CJ and his wife are hopelessly delusional but can do no harm. No one is about to allow him anywhere near a Judge's Bench.

This cannot be said for the optometrist. To live a lie must be quite stressful, not to mention the question of ethics.

Is the explanation for these inventions and re-inventions related to alienation from their new society?

Is it a bid to be noticed, to be credited for what they have achieved? Is it to gain the status they did not have before they left, and certainly, for the majority, did not get in that other country? To gain recognition for the road they have travelled?

That road travelled by the typical returnee was never an easy one. The motherland turned out to be anything but warm and welcoming. There were no streets paved with gold. But there was work, And work they did. They persevered; worked, raised and educated their children, send back remittances to relatives, supporting two economies simultaneously.

They saved and bought a house – the house that was to increase meteorically in value, making many of them more money than they had ever dreamed possible. Moreover, they had contributed to the state pension scheme and their own occupational scheme, so had nest eggs there too.

Back home now and mainly retired, their lives are the antitheses of the one they had lived in rural Jamaica, or in one of the big cities in that other country. They are, at last, financially secure, part of the returnee leisure class, and free to go and come as they please, making the most of their dual citizenship.

Tracing their history from then to now, one can only applaud their tenacity and vision.

One wonders, then, why some feel the need to embellish or reinvent when they are already heroes.

18 YOU GETTING FAT MAN

'You are getting fat, man. What happen to you?'

One would never in a million years get away with saying that to someone in that other country. In fact, only if you want to make an enemy for life would you dare to comment on someone's weight, even if no insult is meant and you are simply stating a fact. At best, you would be considered unforgivably rude, very offensive, completely lacking in manners; or, most likely, all of the above.

In that other country, fat is always a dirty word. To be considered completely beautiful one has to be slim, and a specific size of slimness too.

This preoccupation with slimness is not only to do with health and fitness but has a lot to do with a particular concept of beauty. People are therefore adept at using euphemisms to soften the blow when describing someone considered overweight.

Not so in Jamaica. Here the word comes with a range of meanings and inferences. Indeed, the word is often used without criticism or malice, but simply as an honest observation.

In fact, there is more often than not a liberating fluidity to the use of the word. Sometimes it can be a friendly warning or often an undiluted compliment, especially from those of a certain age. A friend's mother has a church sister who comes from that generation of rural women who did not always have enough. Thin was an outward show of this, fat was the reverse. When my friend visits from that other country, it is always the same dance. The church sister hugs her with delight, pulls back, examines her, and then gushes that she is getting fat. My friend's mother would beg her church sister not to say that 'You are going to make her go on a diet,' she would plead. And since my friend is only a size UK 8, this is always an amusing exchange.

The other day I was with my mechanic. I had only ever known him to be on the plump side. As we spoke, a customer who had clearly not seen him for some time came in. 'You getting fat, man,' she said, surprised. 'What happen to you?' Without a change of expression, no hint of upset, he nodded, 'Yes man. I know. The weight comes on so fast these days.'

With still much of the other country in me I felt the need to ease what I thought an unkind blow, 'Yes, I'm finding that too.' I said, 'It's not always easy to keep slim as we get older.' No one continued the conversation, so superfluous it seemed was my interjection.

Another day I was in a shop. The shop assistant in directing a customer said loudly, 'It's behind that big belly man over there.' The big belly man waved to confirm the location.

Of course, there are many who glory in being slim, who do not accept that being fat is for them. They take pride in, and are admired for, their svelte forms, and work to keep them that way.

Wonderfully, the Jamaican culture does not have a narrow definition of what constitutes a beautiful body.

And this view seems to completely permeate the mindset of many in the society. I used to be taken aback by women who had more than their fair share of fat, yet insisted on wearing overly short skirts, skin-tight jeans and low-cut tops.

These women wear their clothes with liberating ease and do not seem to waste a single moment agonising about a bit of loose flesh here, a bit of flab there.

Fat was once a feminist issue. I wonder how Suzie Orbach would define it now in Jamaica.

19 LIES AND UNTRUTHS

When I was young my grandmother would tell us, my siblings and I, not to use the word lie, but to use the word untruth instead. Granny Bea scorned even the word lie and abhorred liars even more. 'Every liar is a thief, and every thief is a liar,' she would say.

We grew to know that the punishment was always less if we told the truth, and had to learn the poem,

'Speak the truth and speak it ever, cause it what it will...'

Now I wonder whether we were particularly naughty in that area, or whether she was just making sure. In that other country, there was once a big ado about a Cabinet Minister being economical with the truth, to the extent that the term became part of popular culture. It had something to do with a certain statement made by the said politician in Parliament during the *Spycatcher* trial of the 1980s. Apparently, the term was borrowed from someone who had said something similar in the eighteenth century.

So, lies, untruths, and economising with the truth are not new.

Currently, however, there seems to be a total international shift in the perception of telling lies, untruths or being economical with the truth. Or perhaps people are more honest about the norm of lies and lying. Or they have become even more barefaced about it.

Some time ago we were in a restaurant. It was another glorious evening in paradise. We were eating fried fish and other Jamaican delights on the beach when the server brought a dish we had not ordered. When we informed her of this, she immediately launched into a long diatribe, which went along the lines of, 'Yes, you did. You said that you wanted this and that was when I said...' We looked at each other aghast at the immediate, barefaced, and lengthy lie. I suggested that she had the wrong table. She was not to be silenced and continued repeating a conversation she insisted we had had.

One of my friends, visiting from that other country, who does not suffer fools, said, 'That conversation did not happen. You did not have that conversation with anyone at this table.' My friend enunciated every word as she spoke. We felt a bit sorry for the server when she eventually scuttled off with her unordered dish.

Then there was a conversation which went something along these lines:

Client: I sent you an email three weeks ago. I have not had a response

Attorney: I did not get it.

Client: It did not bounce back. I would have had a notification if you had not received it. Have you checked your spam folder?

Attorney: I check it every day, and there is nothing in there from you.

Client (exasperated and disbelieving): I will resend.

A few days later, they had an almost identical conversation so the client resent the email for the third time, and called again.

Attorney: It has just come through.

Client: Which one?

Attorney: The one you sent four weeks ago.

As McEnroe would have said, 'You can't be serious!'

Telling lies seem to be the easiest way to get out of an undesirable situation. Almost everyone, I imagine, has been in such a situation, when rather than hurt a person's feelings or make a person feel bad they resort to lying. Someone I know has an interesting take on it. He often asks, 'Is it a truth that needs to be told?'

Is it a contradiction, though, to suggest that telling lies can be regarded as taking the moral high ground?

Someone else I know distinguishes between what she calls necessary and unnecessary lies. She hates unnecessary lies.

For the highly moral among us, lies are lies and one imagines it will be rare, or at least not habitual for them, to tell either necessary or unnecessary lies. Perhaps if they had to, they would spend time afterwards agonising at having to resort to telling an untruth.

Not so for others. It appears that for an increasing number of people among us, telling lies has shamelessly become an accepted norm.

20 THE HELPER

My ubiquitous good friend, AA, tells me stories about her experiences with staff, and helpers in particular.

She tells me that when she returned home from that other country, she came bubbling with an almost evangelical fervour to give back. Her way of doing so was through giving employment.

She is retired and envisioned four employees in all; housekeeper, cook, personal assistant and gardener.

She had carefully worked out her finances, calculating that as well as paying them what she considered a good living wage and contributing to the Government schemes, she would put in place benefits such as private health insurance and private pension for each worker.

AA says she understood that many of her liberal friends from that other country are sceptical about the idea of domestic staff, especially the idea of a housekeeper. They see it as a relic of an objectionable class-divided society of 'Upstairs Downstairs' fame.

Her first housekeeper was a woman whom one of her friends called 'Bashment Girl' (BG), because of the incredible hairstyles and hair colours that she sported when she came to work, including one that looked like an extended bird's nest coloured red. AA had not mentioned that as one of the *do-not* when she had interviewed BG. The possibility of her thinking that such a hairstyle could be appropriate for work had not crossed her mind, so AA had to let that be. As was her plan from the start, she paid her well over the minimum wage and all, apart from the loudness of the hairstyles, BG seemed to be fine.

About three months into her employment, BG brought six book lists for each of her six children to

AA. My friend said she looked them over and made what she considered appropriate noises, believing that BG thought she would be interested to see what her children would be doing at school.

AA thought BG looked nonplussed as she returned the book lists to her, but as she was still learning about what were now new cultural mannerisms, she put it down to another thing lost in translation. Later, after BG had left for the day, she got a call from BG's live-in lover, the father, AA understood, of her two youngest children. He said, 'I have to tell you, despite de big money you paying her, an de adda tings yu give her, you are a mean woman. You can do even better than dat. In your farin money, de book dem caass noting.'

Shocked by the effrontery, my friend gave BG two weeks' pay when she next appeared at work, and asked her not to return, promptly changing her mobile number too.

Then there was the gardener who seemed fascinated with running water, and would let it gush through the hose with gay abandon. The gardener was illiterate so AA had hired a weekly reading teacher for him and asked the teacher to help her to remind him about the importance of not wasting water.

It was all to no avail. When she reminded the gardener yet again not to waste water, he promptly put down the hose, the water still flowing liberally, and said, 'Me gwaan leave you job you know. Me no like woman tell, tell me wey fe do.'

The gardener was true to his word; he did not return to work the following Monday. Incidentally, she said she saw him over a year later. Unabashed, he asked her if she still had his job, as he had not found another one since he left her.

AA says she now uses the national papers to advertise for housekeeping staff. Recently, after taking calls for a week or so, it struck her that almost everyone gave the same response when asked why she had left her previous job. Ninety per cent had been looking after an elderly person who had now died. Nine percent had been working for families who had migrated or returned to their home country. None of them, therefore, could provide any references from a recent employer.

My favourite of all her stories was the live-in housekeeper who had a spun a lengthy tale about a lung operation she had which necessitated almost two-monthly re-admissions to the hospital, ranging from a few days to one week. AA liked her and did not want to lose her, so she told her she would keep the job open for her, and paid her in full when she was away.

After six months, she decided to visit the live-in housekeeper in the hospital. This was a couple of parishes away from where my friend lived, so she decided to make a weekend of it, especially as the housekeeper lived near the stunning south coast of the island.

When AA got to the hospital, her housekeeper was nowhere to be found, and moreover, the nurses on the hospital ward had never heard of her housekeeper. Thinking she had the wrong hospital, even the wrong parish, AA called the housekeeper's daughter, whom she had listed as her next of kin. It all unravelled after that. There had been no lung operation and no hospital admissions. Rather, she was a part-time farmer, growing mainly carrots, and had to do something or other every two months or so, and her weekends off seemingly were not enough.

AA thought she had to be doing something wrong, especially when she heard of people who retained staff for years. As her knowledge grew, she found she was not alone. There seemed to be more experiences like her own, than the converse.

When the farmer-come-housekeeper came to take her belongings, AA wanted to know why she had not just told her, and negotiated.

'My grandmother says find a fool, deal with him,' the housekeeper said simply.

Now AA says, with a little sadness, that she only employs a gardener for one day a week and does her housework and her other duties herself. She says she saves the money she would have paid the staff and invests it for her already well-looked-after grandchildren, and her favourite international charities.

21 PROFESSIONAL FUNERAL-GOERS

I read recently that in Taiwan families often employ professional mourners to capture and demonstrate the grief and loss felt by a family at the death of a loved one.

The professional mourners perform their role with superlative fervour and passion, the aim being to capture and demonstrate the intensity of the pain felt by the family.

Taiwanese families pay heavily for this service.

In Jamaica, funerals are big business too, not only for the funeral directors but for the professional funeral-goers, and there is, it seems, at least, one if not several of them in every district.

Someone I know, WF, recently stopped to pick up a man thumbing a lift. He was near a throng of people who were clearly at an after-funeral event. The man was dressed in a black suit, white shirt and black bow tie. He carried the unmistakable box dinner discreetly packaged in a plastic bag. He seemed by all accounts to be desperate for the lift.

WF asked him why the hurry, especially when they were in a part of Jamaica where few knew the meaning of the word hurry. 'I am coming from a funeral,' he said.

'Oh', said WF, not sure how that merited hurrying, but asking instead, 'Who's died?'

The man hesitated. 'Not sure,' he said.

'Oh. So where are you going now?' asked WF.

'To another funeral,' he said. WF did not feel he should ask if he knew whose funeral that was.

There are those in areas all over Jamaica, whose ears are finely attuned to the news of deaths and funerals. Many seem to come alive at the news of death.

I experienced that myself when my father died many years ago. During the period from the announcement of his death to the day of his burial, individuals appeared at my parents' home whom we barely knew, and many whom we had never set eyes on before. They came expecting, and received, copious amounts of food and drinks for the fourteen days from the announcement of the death to the funeral.

Some traditions in Jamaica seem to encourage the feasting surrounding deaths, funerals, and professional funeral-going.

There is, for instance, the tradition of visiting the dead house, as the home of the deceased is called.

As soon as the news of the death spreads, especially in rural areas, those vaguely connected, as well as friends and families, appear. They do so to give face-to-face condolences to the family, but also to get their share of the inevitable and plentiful food and drinks on offer; beginning perhaps with fried fish and bread, fried chicken and bread, plus white rice, curried goat and salads of all descriptions on the last and final day.

Indeed, the days from the death to the day of the funeral can be likened to a marathon of callers, feasting and domino-playing.

As a child, in the glorious hills of Saint Catherine, I grew up knowing that the dead house was not to be empty of callers until the deceased was laid to rest. So vivid were the stories of the need for such post-death gatherings and feasting, I imagined the spirit lingering in his old yard to ensure all the traditions were followed, leaving to eternity only after the final day of post-burial feasting.

In that District, there were three special days of feasting for the dead. Firstly there was Nine Nights, aptly named as this occurred nine nights after the death. In those glorious hills of Saint Catherine, that night was especially marked as the whole District would attend and there would be much recitation of memories of the dead, renditions of songs, and playing of banjos, flutes and mouth organs. It was not unknown for a goat to be killed for the Nine Nights feasting.

The second of the three special nights was the Set-up. That traditionally occurred on the night before the funeral, when those who could, would spend the entire night rendering their dirges for the dead, and, of course, eating and drinking. The Christians sometimes hijacked a part, if not all of that night, for a prayer meeting. That was never, however, to the exclusion of the feasting.

Finally on the day of the funeral and after the burial, there was the glorious climax, the after-burial feast. One could not imagine a funeral without the eating and drinking that traditionally followed.

Families could gain or lose their reputation according to what they provided on that day and the numbers they fed and supplied with food and drink.

Importantly, it was not enough to feed those present; the bereaved family had to have enough for mourners to take away for those who were not able to attend.

I attended a funeral recently which brought back memories of those days, so many years ago in those glorious hills. On leaving the church, I overheard a couple of women whose homes were adjacent to the church discussing where the after-burial feast was to be held and making plans to attend with their children.

'You know who dead?' one asked her friend.

'I don't know for sure. Someone said it's dat woman who used to drive pass in de white car.'
With that, they went off, to don their funeral garb to attend the burial feast.

22 THE REAL JAMAICA VIA MY MOTHER'S EXTRAORDINARY HATS

A few years ago I invited a friend from that other country to travel to Jamaica with us. We stayed for two weeks in Montego Bay doing tourist-type things.

The remaining two weeks we spent at my parents' home. My friend, ML, was well-travelled and discerning, and moreover was part of the thinking class. So, although she loved beaches, especially as getting a tan was a necessary part of travelling to the tropics, sunbathing could never be the whole holiday. She wanted to see the real Jamaica. She often said so as we planned and looked forward to the trip, and after we had arrived on the island.

This thing, about the real Jamaica, intrigues me. You hear this statement often from visitors to the island. You may be with visitors on one of the stunning beaches, on a golf course beside the sea, in a modern architecturally-designed mansion, in one of the so-called high-end areas, or even in one of the spectacular shopping centres or malls. They invariably say as they bask in the beauty of it all, this does not feel like Jamaica or this reminds me of...and they name a famous and glamorous place in the country to our north.

Their disbelief suggests they cannot imagine that Jamaica has many sides, and think, it seems, that only the downtrodden, the poor, the sufferers constitute the real Jamaica. The successful, the affluent, the educated middle and upper classes, even the genteel poor, could not possibly be part of the real Jamaica.

That being said, my friend ML was, and still is, completely free of malice or ill-will. Being well-travelled and well-educated, she knew the diversity and range that constitutes any society, First World or Third World.

After our time in Montego Bay, my mother generously took a day off work and collected us from our hotel.

After we had spent the first day recovering from the journey from Montego Bay to glorious Saint Catherine, I set out to show ML the real Jamaica.

We went to beaches, parks, waterfalls, and natural spas. We visited historic buildings and went to see residential areas of all kinds, both urban and rural.

We explored restaurants, bars and hotels to eat and just hang out. ML especially wanted to see beaches that the locals use and the downtown areas she has heard about in Reggae songs, especially those by Bob Marley and Culture, Trench Town and Ferry Police Station, for example.

Interestingly, she much preferred the rough and ready (as it was then) beach of Hellshire to what she described as the sanitised ones we had visited on the north coast. Even now, over twenty years later, she still talks about the baked lobster and fried fish platter we had there that day.

There were many extraordinary days but the most extraordinary one for ML was what she called her glimpse of Edwardian England, by way of my mother's dress style.

The first time she saw my mother dressed for Sunday Church, she exclaimed audibly. It reminded her, she said, of women dressed for Ascot or some such Meet; well-tailored clothes, hat, shoes and bag to match. She especially liked my mother's hats, most seemingly handmade.

My mother, nervous about us discovering downtown by ourselves as we wanted to do, spotted the solution. She suggested that we went with her instead to her milliner, and she would go via the areas ML wanted to see.

Eventually, in the shop ML went into raptures, saying it brought back memories of her grandmother and similar journeys she had made with her. We spent ages watching women coming in to be measured and fitted and to peruse hats of all descriptions.

On the way back to that other country, I asked ML whether she had discovered the real Jamaica, 'Of course...' she said with a wry smile, '...baked lobster at Hellshire beach, and your mother's extraordinary hats.'

23 UNFINISHED BUILDINGS

You do not have to spend a long time in Jamaica to notice that there are numerous buildings in various stages of incompletion in almost every area; churches, offices, warehouses and would-be family homes.

Some of the family homes are occupied by individuals who are taking their time to build their dream home or even their simple abode, and are seeking to do so without burdensome mortgages. They seem content to live in a partially-finished house as they slowly earn the funds to complete it. This can take months, years, or even a decade.

As there are houses going up around families, there are unfinished buildings with no occupants in sight. Buildings left lonely and dreary; a feature, if not a blight, on every community, modest or high-end.

A few years ago, we were spending a weekend with someone we know in glorious Saint Catherine, and going for an early morning stroll through the area.

Punctuating wonderfully-designed houses of all shapes and sizes were unfinished houses in various degrees of incompletion.

Some had seemingly been there for so long they had taken on the form of ancient ruins. Others had trees, flowers and creepers of all descriptions growing in them. A herd of donkeys had even invaded one of the houses. We were amused that in each of the six would-be rooms downstairs, a donkey grazed happily as if that was the most natural thing in the world.

People who do not know better no doubt stand in judgement over those who seem to start these buildings, only to abandon them, no thought of the impact on neighbours and communities. Why did they not get accredited professionals? Why did they not get a quantity surveyor to price the job beforehand so they knew how to budget? Why did they not get an honest architect, reputable contractor, structural and electrical engineers?

Then they hear the stories, too often to ignore, and it dawns on them that the problem is not usually with the poor unfortunate owners. 'It lies with jinnal* contractors and their bands of professional thieves,' RK informed me, speaking from bitter experience.

RK is from a particular group that frequently falls prey to this unscrupulous band. Like the ubiquitous unfinished buildings, stories abound of the woeful experiences of returnees at their hands.

'They always build your house, and another house out of your materials,' a returnee forced to live in a partially-finished house told me.

Ignorant of the situation I defended them, 'They have to make a profit.'

Only later did I realise that he meant it literally; that materials would be over-bought, one set for you and one for them, and would disappear off site, in-situ security guards or not.

There are countless other tricks of the trade too, designed to part the returnees from their funds. The architect makes errors in the drawings. The excited, romantic returnee, too trusting, too lost in the joy of returning, does not notice. During the building process, he is told there has to be this and that variation and everyone in the chain has to be paid for the variation; the architect, the quantity surveyor (QS) and, of course, the contractor.

Then it dawns on them that everyone is in cahoots, and the hapless owners are the only ones out of the circle. Eventually, they find that they are getting less than they paid for, pine instead of the cedar shown on the plans and priced by the QS, and untreated soil, so termites silently rip through their home, easily devouring the untreated pine. This is despite the fact that termite treatment at various stages of the construction has already been priced in the Bills of

Quantities, certified as properly carried out by the supervising architect, and so paid for.

Worse still, the contractor walks off the job, demanding more money for materials that he says have escalated in price, despite provisions in the Bills of Quantities for such increases, and of course despite the signed Contract. The returnee, now fully down to earth, is left with an unfinished house, with no more funds to continue. Some retrace their steps to that other country. Others, having no such option, do the best they can and join the countless others who live in unfinished, sub-standard houses.

A labourer, hearing one of these returnees complaining about having been mercilessly robbed by his contractor, laughed heartily, 'You think they finish with you? They not finish with you yet.' He emphasised, 'They rob the likes of you twice. When they building your house, they jinnal you and overcharge you. And when you die they capture your property because your kids won't want to come and live out here.'

*Jinnal - A Jamaican word that roughly means confidence trickster, or the art of confidence trickery.

24 I DON'T WORK FOR BABYLON

My friend AG is a natural when it comes to repartee. She is never short of the right response and often leaves us in hysterics when she takes on unsuspecting souls who try to outwit her.

Long before she was a returnee, she used to visit her parents almost annually. She came, like most others from that other country, suffused with sympathy and more than a little guilt about those who seemed less fortunate, and who did not have the opportunities she had.

At the corner of her parents' road, she said, there was usually a group of young men sitting idly on a wall. Each time she passed them, they would beg her money. She took to carrying money just for them.

Eventually, she said to them, 'I am a middle-aged woman; you are young. Why aren't you working, or, at least, trying to find a job? Why are you just sitting here?'

'Me?' One of them responded. 'I don't work for Babylon. I will never work for Babylon.'

'I have to work for Babylon,' she said, 'and this money is Babylon's money, and yesterday was the last time you got some of Babylon's money from me.'

Some individuals on the island certainly seem to have a puzzling relationship to employment. Many who are ostensibly desperate for income to raise their families out of poverty, to enable their children to get a good education, to enable improved living conditions, are the very ones who are seemingly work-resistant.

Many factors conspire to maintain this status quo. There is, for instance, the remittance culture.

Remittances from abroad have a laudable history. Parents who had to go abroad to work would send funds to relatives to care for the children they had left behind. Most often, these were ageing grandparents who continued to be subsistence farmers and market sellers as well as surrogate parents to their grandchildren, so hard working were they.

Those days are now mainly gone as it seems, is the culture of hard work and self-reliance that was characteristic of that period. What has replaced it for some is the culture of begging and dependency. Family members who go abroad for some reason seem to believe that by having travelled, they are financially responsible for those left at home. Those left behind seem to encourage that belief.

A gardener I know was recently bemoaning the fact that his young sister had tragically died in the USA. She was the youngest of seven he said, was a mother of five children, and had an ageing father who needed several different kinds of medication. He expressed the sadness you would expect at a sister's death but he ended with, 'She was our source, what are we going to do now?' I asked what he meant. He said that since she had migrated she had made it her duty to send money for everyone in the family on a monthly basis.

'Even if it was small, she never forgot her responsibility.'

I suggested that it must have been stressful for her to be supporting twelve people, especially adults who are able to work.

'No,' he said, 'she managed it. She had three jobs over there in foreign.'

The young man seemed completely comfortable with the fact that his sister had to work three jobs to support him and his adult siblings.

Returnees and visitors also unwittingly perpetuate this culture of dependency and work resistance. They are invariably woven tales of hardship and desperation by people they meet. Many return to their countries having made guilt-fused commitments to send funds to help.

Undoubtedly, there are families and individuals who are in need of charity and deserve whatever help they can get. Equally, it seems, there are many who can help themselves, but who have the greatest sense of entitlement about what others should do for them.

Another friend told me that the day she took over a new office, a young security guard approached her. He had not met her before but immediately asked if she would buy him lunch.

She challenged him. 'You come from foreign,' he defended himself. 'It's easier to make money over there. When you come back, you have to share it.'

'Why should I buy you, a working young man, lunch?' she asked him. 'If I have to buy someone lunch it would be someone who has no job.' He mumbled under his breath that she was mean and bad-minded. She challenged him. 'You come from foreign,' he defended himself. 'It's easier to make money over there. When you come back, you have to share it.'

25 GREETINGS

When I first returned to Jamaica, I was reprimanded several times by people who were outraged that I could enter a room and not greet those who were already there, or pass people in certain situations and not speak to them.

The first such was in a doctor's office. I walked in, reported to the receptionist, sat down and took out my book. Only seconds later did I realise that the thrown words* were meant for me. I was being labelled rude, without manners and the like. Oops, I thought, I forgot to say good morning again.

Then there was the security guard at a friend's son's school. One week she asked me to do the evening school run for her. I duly parked, walked to the gate and waited there for BA to be released. It was only on the last day that I heard that the security guard had complained I had disrespected him by never greeting him.

In the island, you are expected to be aware of the appropriate greeting at every time of day, and be ready to extend the correct salutation: be it morning, afternoon, evening or night. The latter is especially interesting to me. I was used to saying 'good night' only to my nearest and dearest when about to turn in for the night. Not so in Jamaica. On leaving your office or an area late in the evening, it is standard to wish good night to anyone vaguely familiar.

Charming, you may think. Indeed, I found it charming on a recent visit to the British Virgin Islands when school pupils greeted me and stepped aside to let me pass. That aspect of old-world charm has left urban Jamaica, though not, I understand, rural

Jamaica. It is the habit of greeting all and sundry that remains steadfast throughout the island.

In that other country, random individuals and groups do not wait expectantly for those new to the group to greet them. Indeed, it is clearly not the case either in some other parts of Europe.

In Lisbon, I headed out of my room across the cobbled courtyard and into the dining room for breakfast, passing fellow guests seemingly from all parts of Europe enjoying their breakfast in the sun. I bade a general good morning as I passed the tables. I was not conscious of responses as I was purposeful in my stride, anxious to eat as quickly as possible and to start my exploration of the city. In the smaller dining room, I extended greetings again, with a Jamaican-like accompanying slight raise of the hand. The only responses I clocked were from the two workers, and a mature gentleman eating with his female companion.

I quickly re-learnt that it was quite fine to pass individuals, small or large groups that you see every morning at breakfast and not breathe a word of greeting. Six years of re-learnt habits die hard, however, so like a tic, the greeting would still escape each morning periodically. To be fair, one or two smiled hesitantly, not sure whether to humour my madness or not, or throw caution to the wind and smile fully or even respond audibly.

Then there was the group of elderly locals I passed each morning sitting together on Travessa do Terreiro a Santa Catarina. They were there every morning as I set out on my way to Largo do Chiado to amble, to catch the metro or tram, to see yet another side of the city, or find the out-of-the-way vegetarian restaurant. I decided to fight my instinct and not breathe a word of greeting to them. Difficult and unnatural though it felt, I managed it.

151

Then I came to a group of young men, one of whom had jumped up, greeted me and helped me with my luggage when the taxi driver had deposited me too far from the apartments on my first day in the city, the road to the correct spot unexpectedly closed. I was delighted to see him and his group again, to repeat my thanks. My Portuguese is limited to four or five words, and even fewer sentences, and their English about the same. Obrigada being one of the words I knew, I voiced it with confidence. We compared countries of origin; Guinea and Angola, they said. When I said, I was from Jamaica, that sent them into raptures of recognition and obvious delight. They each repeated the name Jamaica several times, as if in song, then one said 'reggae,' the other 'Bob Marley,' another 'Shaggy, Rasta and Bolt' in that order, as if rehearsed.

Wow, I thought, basking in the warmth of their friendship and their obvious fascination with a culture they had only experienced second-hand.

I looked forward to meeting them each morning and sometimes in the evenings. At times they were all there, sometimes only one of them. But there were always the lively greetings; Bom dia, from them, Hi or Hello from me, until eventually we greeted in unison: Bom dia. Até logo.

*Mildly abusive words meant to be heard but not said directly to a person.

26 STREET- SELLERS - NOT ONLY IN JAMAICA

I was wandering leisurely along the road bordering the Giudecca Canal in Venice. I was going up and down yet another set of steps when I heard what sounded like a herd of elephants behind me. Before I had time to turn, about twelve men of mainly Asian and two of African descent rushed past, as I pinned myself to the side of the bridge. Others around me did the same or stood still in their tracks.

Most of the men had rolls of cream-coloured bundles. A couple, the two of African descent, had strings of bags, bearing the logos of expensive well-known brands, slung over their shoulders.

Those with the less burdensome bundles took the lead as they scampered along the canal. Suddenly they turned left onto a side road. One of them, the tallest and biggest, and with the largest string of bags, had been bringing up the rear the entire time. As his co-workers disappeared around buildings, a man suddenly jumped down the steps and grabbed hold of the straggler. There was a struggle and a lot of fast-spoken Italian.

The man who had hold of him was apparently persuading him to stand still. Some onlookers thought he was a thief but were put right by someone who seemed in the know. 'Undercover cops,' she said. 'They have fake goods, and have no licence to sell here.' For some reason, that information immediately changed the atmosphere among the onlookers who had seemed nervous at the sudden chase and capture. One responded, 'I suppose they have to make a living somehow.' A few grunted agreement but most just watched as the struggle continued. Someone tried to take pictures. 'No photos,' the police shouted. 'No photos,' others echoed from among the onlookers. A few minutes later another plain-clothes policeman came charging down the steps, obviously not as fit as the sellers or his colleague. He seemed angry at having being made to run. He furiously collected the bags that had fallen like leaves from the seller's shoulder, and struggling with his designer load, brought up the rear as the seller was finally subdued and frog-marched out of sight.

For some reason, I felt incredibly sad for the seller. Why had he not thrown the bags away to give himself more chance of escape?

The following day, this time around the St. Mark's Square area, I was conscious of the relatively large number of the informal sellers; touting bags, leather goods and toys that splattered when thrown to the ground. There were plenty of uniformed police around but the men went on selling, gently persuading passers-by to part with their cash.

As evening fell, I was exhausted from wandering but was unable to pull myself away. I noticed that there was a cat-and-mouse game being played between the police and the sellers. As well as watching for potential buyers, they were clearly watching to see whether the police would continue to turn a blind eye.

A police officer would walk as if towards them; the sellers would partially roll up their selling mats, or crouch down low, ready it seemed to make a dash for it. No action from the police; they unrolled, stood up straight and continued their persuasive lyrics. One called to me. 'I have no money,' I said, used to Jamaica sellers' lyrics. 'You don't have to,' he replied persuasively, 'let's talk.' He smiled. I returned the smile and walked on.

I had told NK about the chasing incident; she had been amused so I wanted to take pictures of one of them to show her, minus face of course, with bags, strung across his body. That proved impossible.

The sellers turned out to be very much like those who sell around traffic lights in Jamaica. There cannot be a more alert group of entrepreneurs. They are super-aware of potential buyers. If you twitch as your car stops at the lights, they rush over to you, thinking you may be going for cash. In the same way, the San Marco sellers would instinctively sense attention and turn immediately. After all, the transaction had to be quick; more than that, if you prove to be an undercover cop, they have to be able to secure their goods, pack up shop and make a run for it.

'They should get one of the mats the sellers in

South London have,' NK said, 'the one-sweep-and-I'm-gone mat. Or,' she added, 'develop the cunning of those in downtown Mobay. One minute they're in full swing selling all sorts. They spy a cop and they're off, nonchalantly sauntering down the road, goods having disappeared into thin air.'

27 MISUNDERSTANDINGS

Someone I know, ND, called a business in Kingston to ask its email address. A staff member responded,

'nameofbusiness.com.'

ND said, 'That would be the website. What's the email address?' The staff member repeated,

'Nameofbusiness.com!'

ND, in turn, emphasised, 'That is not an email address.'

'Mi sey! Naeemm aff business dat cumm!'

ND, exasperated, said, 'That cannot be an email address. The email address needs to have @...'

The staff member kissed her teeth and put the phone down. ND redialled and asked to speak to someone else. The staff member put her on hold. Two minutes or so later, someone else came to the phone.

ND explained what she needed. She also said that she took exception to the response of the previous staff member. 'There was a misunderstanding,' the new staff member said.

'There was a misunderstanding,' is a widely-used get out clause in Jamaica. Some individuals are incapable of accepting responsibility for their error, rudeness or poor customer service, and more often than not use that phase to place responsibility in this amorphous realm.

People I know seem to have experienced their fair share of them.

There was, for example, the government worker, GW, who refused to allow EF to register to vote at the office, she attended. She had never heard of the area where EF lived, she said. EF showed her the area on the map. 'Nobody lives up there,' the worker stated categorically and turned away to continue her conversation with her co-worker.

EF could not persuade her of the existence of her area, or that individuals could register at any electoral office on the island. She dismissed EF, giving her the address that she insisted was the correct office. EF went to the office but also wrote a letter of complaint.

It was six months before she knew that a manager had received her letter.

GW was herself kept in the dark until her annual review. The manager called EF during the interview, thanked her for her letter, and immediately handed the phone to GW. It was clear even on the phone that GW had not been given time to recover from the shock of a letter of complaint unveiled at her annual review. However, she composed herself sufficiently to say, 'I am sorry for what happened; it was a misunderstanding...'

One of my favourite misunderstanding stories is that of the gate man. The electronics on LD's gate needed attention. Wary of getting someone at random out of the book, LD asked another tradesman. He recommended SM.

SM seemed knowledgeable and immediately diagnosed the problem. SM quoted his rate for labour and another rate for parts. As her tried-and-trusted electrician had recommended him, LD paid him in advance for the labour and the amount he said the parts would cost.

Each day when he had said he would return passed with one excuse after another. Finally, the gateman arrived and completed the work, but without the receipt for the parts or the labour. Even more, he quoted a new rate for labour and insisted that she had not paid him.

Only when LD produced the cheque stub did he relent.

LD insisted that she needed her receipt for labour and the tax receipt for the parts. Many days and several calls later, he brought the receipts for parts and labour. The latter was hand-written on what appeared to be discarded headed paper. The figures matched the disputed revised amount for parts. My friend called the shop to verify.

The manager knew nothing of that kind of receipt, as tax receipts would never be hand-written.

My friend called the gate man and upbraided him for trying to rob her. 'It's a misunderstanding,' he said. 'It's only a simple misunderstanding.'

28 BIG HOUSE

I was at a *dead house*; a friend's husband had died that day in a car accident. As was the tradition, friends went to his home to be with his family. The news was getting around so people were coming and going. JB was a successful local businessman who grew up in the area and everybody knew him.

There was an inner circle of friends who sat at one end of the pool deck. They were not just passing by. They were there to stay for the evening, and had each brought a bottle and food; jerk pork, jerk chicken, ackee and salt fish, patties and cod fish fritters. Since JB had only just died, the family had not yet got into the rhythm. The children and grandchildren would be arriving from their various homes in the US and the

UK from the next day. Soon they would organise extra staff to cook and to serve drinks. The fire would not go out until after the burial, nor would the drinks stop flowing.

The circle of friends sat around talking with K, JB's wife, remembering her husband, expressing shock and disbelief and berating the dangerous drivers in the island.

K was distant most of the time, but everyone understood and only occasionally filled her glass with red wine, or tried to encourage her to eat something.

The fact that the subject came round to returnees was a surprise. That the story went on as long as it did was even more so.

I was the only returnee present.

'I don't mean you, but why do the returnees build such big houses when they come to Jamaica?' DM asked, as if to the group, but looking steadily at me. Since I was not an authority on the subject, I shrugged and looked in K's direction, wondering if she would think that subject inappropriate. She did not seem to hear the question.

The other three in the group sipped their red wine for several moments before anyone responded.

CC, a good friend of the deceased, spoke thoughtfully, 'I suppose it's because they lived in those small terraced houses in England, or in council flats.'

'I can't imagine that anyone who lived in a council house in England would ever be able to build or buy a big house here,' I said, struggling to control my irritation.

'But I don't understand it,' DM persisted. 'Half of them can't even speak English correctly, but they live in these big houses.'

Not sure of the connection between the ability to speak English well and living in big houses, I said, 'I suppose, like you, they have a right to spend their money in the way they see fit. They have worked for it, after all.'

DM is educated, well-travelled, and ostensibly sensible. Something else must be going on there, I thought. Alas, I'm not a psychologist.

She told the story of someone she knew. No one interrupted her as she spoke. I tried to guess who she might be referring to. It is a small place.

RB and RR are married. He is about 10 years older than her. He has lived in England since he was a little boy; she migrated when she was in her teens.

They decided to build a house in Jamaica soon after they met and married. It was the second marriage for both of them, and both had several children and grandchildren.

They came on holiday and decided on an area on the North coast where land was being sold by the lot. (A lot is always somewhere less than an acre.) They bought four adjoining lots to form their plot.

Their plot is in an area with one of those seductive Jamaican names. It is several hundred feet above sea level with an 180 degree view of the alluring Caribbean Sea.

It is about a mile from the other lavish houses in the area, and so high above them that only their tops are visible. The varying shades of green that span the area between the houses and the sea captivated them every time they visited.

As they drove to their plot, before their house was finished, the significance of the big bad dogs behind the high-fenced, heavily-gated, security monitored homes was lost on them.

In the ten years, it took them to build their twenty thousand square feet home; they did not stop once to ask why the last house in the area was so far from theirs, or why the electricity supply, water and asphalted road stopped at this last house too.

Moreover, they had never ventured beyond the border of their land in the other direction.

They planted copious amounts of fruit trees as the house went up, and envisioned lounging with friends and family by their Olympic-sized pool on lazy days, and spending long evenings barbecuing and eating anything the land gave.

Their pool is an engineering feat in itself. The house is built on the highest part of their land, but they wanted the pool on the top floor so that their vision of the sea would be unhindered.

The house is on three floors with fifteen en-suite bedrooms, powder rooms on every side of the house, several family rooms, an octagonal kitchen and a dining room, which flows onto the pool deck.

They imagined lots of dinner parties beside the pool, so they designed the house to allow visitors access to the upper pool deck without having to go through the house. The pool deck is also self-contained, with its own bar area, kitchenette and powder rooms. There are two prominent barbecues at the edge of the deck; an imported electrical one and a local jerk pan made from corrugated iron. They barbecue freshly-caught fish at least once a week.

RR dabbled in interior design and spared no expense in creating the interiors of her dream home.

She boasted of using designer paints, fabrics and the most expensive kitchen appliances she could import. Her impeccable, expensive taste is undeniable.

She readily admits now, that importing appliances with sixty cycles when Jamaica operates on fifty cycles, and with frequent surges and power cuts, was one of their many mistakes.

The ten years of planning, building and furnishing, though arduous, including manoeuvring their way around opportunist and dishonest contractors, turned out in retrospect to be the best years for her. At least, then they still had their home in England. They alternated trips to supervise the building. For the ten years, they were suffused with unquenchable hope and optimism. They would be moving back home.

By the time the house was finally built and furnished, they had sold their businesses and rental properties they owned, and dug deep into their savings. They withdrew what remained, closed all their bank accounts and opened new ones in the land of their birth. The fixed deposit interest rates were relatively high so they would live on the interest they gained. RR's pensions would be a bonus. BR's pension was a few years away.

Their justification for their big house was their children, grandchildren and friends. They foresaw people staying with them every other month, if not every month.

The family and friends do come, but far less frequently than they had imagined.

Some of the friends who come see it as a cheap holiday. They deposit their luggage, spread themselves out in the house, and use utilities with gay abandon.

They cannot understand that Jamaican electricity is one of the most expensive in the world, costing more each month than many of their mortgages. They think her a cheapskate for turning off lights after them and frowning at the continual use of the air-conditioners.

BR complains that these friends think nothing of sandwiching their cost-free days staying with her, with costly days at all-inclusive hotels. She seethes but cannot speak her mind. Those who do offer to pay leave her feeling guilty and offended. The thoughtful few bring gifts; try not to overburden the helper by helping out and take them out to meals as a thank you for having them.

However kind or helpful the guests, she is exhausted when they leave; but then the house resonates with silence and she finds herself longing for others to visit.

Secretly she wonders at their madness. What had possessed them? What they could do now with all the money they had spent on building and furnishing!

They think of running a business from their home, registering it as a bed and breakfast perhaps. But since they have now found that they are only a few miles from a troubled area, they know that would present difficulties, if not to the registering authorities then to them. They would not want their guests to hear the burst of gunshots as they occasionally did.

When they were alone, they locked up most of the rooms, confining their living to their bedroom and dining area only, but spending most of their time on the deck by the pool. That was some compensation – but not enough for her.

BR feels isolated. She joins the Returning

Residents' Association, but finds she had little in common with the members. She complains that she would not have been friends with them abroad either.

She says she finds them simple-minded, envious and unfriendly.

There is an even bigger gulf between her and the locals. It seems everything they say or do irritate, annoys and frustrates her. How can they not see that this or that is wrong? Why can't they change and do things as she is used to them being done? When will they stop behaving like that? How, why, and when, are the words she uses most often.

She takes to shunning returnees and locals alike, but they shun her too. The returnees say she takes on airs and graces, behaving as if she is better them. The locals say, with a sneer, that they know the district from which she came.

RR is immune from it all. He wears the permanent smile of deep contentment. He often says with a hearty laugh, 'the elements were perfectly lined up when I decided to come back home.' He makes friends easily, frequents restaurants and bars, never misses a music or stage show, and is a member of at least two domino clubs and various interest groups. He enjoys touring the island, like the big shot he considers he is.

He enjoys pretty young girls flirting with him, and he loves being addressed as *sir* by men and women alike. Occasionally he is seen with one of the pretty young girls in his pick-up truck. But that type of behaviour is no surprise to anyone.

The bank interest rate has decreased drastically now, and his pension barely keeps them afloat. But what can they do? All their investments are tied up in the big house. At least, his pension goes further than it would do abroad, he consoles his wife.

Their house was broken into recently. She had turned the monitored alarm system off when her husband left for one of his clubs and had forgotten to put it back on. She was there alone with the helper.

The burglars must have been watching them. One minute she was in the dining room doing something or other, the next minute two men were standing over her with guns.

She could not get to the panic button to summon the armed security guards. The gunmen were in the house for hours, tormenting and threatening her, taking everything they could. Luckily, they did not physically harm her or her helper. The mental scars, she says, are indelible. Worse than physical harm, she insists.

Her misery grows by the day. She quarrels with her husband about the house. She tells RR they have to sell. She can only stay in Jamaica if they can move to another area, to a smaller house in a gated community, one where she can feel safer.

RR will not have it. They went through too much building the house and have come too far since then, he insists.

BR is finding it hard to sleep. She has seen the doctor. He says she is depressed and prescribes tranquilizers for her.

RR is tired of her gloominess. He puts the house on the market to please her. He knows it will never sell, not for what they are asking. What they have to ask to break even, let alone make a profit. Besides, who would want such a massive house?

It has been three years now since they moved to Jamaica for good. BR has turned sixty and has qualified for her occupational, though not her state pension.

By the time she received her first pension cheque she had made her decision; she would go back to England. If her husband did not want to go back with her, she would have to leave him. She would stay with one of her children. Hopefully, she would eventually get some help from the Government to find a studio flat or, as she gets older, supported lodgings.

RR did not flinch when she told him her decision. He was expecting it, wishing it, so he was relieved. He organised the shipping of her belongings, helped her to pack when the day came and drove her to the airport.

There was no ceremony and certainly no tears, just brief goodbyes.

She occasionally visits to see him and the house, but those visits are getting fewer and fewer, further and further apart.

29 QUARRELS

Public quarrelling is a feature of Jamaican society. One often stumbles upon blazing rows; ferocious gesticulating, loud voices, curses and threats. It unsettles and scares a lot of returnees until they have experienced a few of them for themselves.

I was waiting in line in the bank. The queue looped inside a rope barrier, guiding customers towards the cashiers, who as always were taking their time with no incentive to get through the line in a hurry.

I had not been in the country long; I knew that this was a characteristic of banks but was irritated and frustrated nonetheless. I looked around for facial expressions of support but everyone was relaxed, lost in their own thoughts. I took out my novel and tried to read, but I was too angry to concentrate. How could they get away with keeping everyone waiting for so long?

A very thin, tall man, dressed in worn but clean clothes, entered the bank talking at the top of his voice. He did not join the queue but paced up and down, with each step his voice getting louder and louder. A few of the customers sniggered and went back to their thoughts, unperturbed.

There was no reaction from either the security guard posted at the door or the one who held his position in the middle of the bank. I frowned. What the hell was going on?

The thin man continued gesticulating and cursing, accusing the bank of stealing his money. He said cash he had deposited had not been recorded in his book.

'Just because me can't read, oounnu tink oounnu can rob me. Me come fe me money. Me want me money!' he shouted, emphasising every word as he paced up and down, his tone more frenzied by the minute.

Uneasy that it might escalate, I watched the security guards, the cashiers, the Customer Services desk, expecting, hoping for someone to intervene and calm him down.

'Me sey! Me waant me money! Oounnu teef me money!' he screamed, holding his deposit book aloft.

The disturbance went on for minutes, or so it seemed to me. The few customers who had sniggered lost interest, oblivious and uncaring of his rant. I alone seemed concerned.

In that other country he would most certainly have been ejected, the police called, possibly resulting in him being sectioned under the Mental Health Act, I thought. I tried not to look at him. I did not want to catch his eye and for him to try and draw me into his story, as he tried unsuccessfully to do to other customers.

Eventually, there was silence and I turned cautiously to see a bank staff member talking to him. She was talking quietly, but his response, though now calmer, was still loud. 'Me see now. Oh, so de amount is here. Me never know. You right, dat is what me put in. Dat it what me have.' Satisfied, but wanting to have the last word he shouted to all who would listen. 'Dem know me ignorant, so dem know dat aldoe me can't read or write, them can't teef me money.'

With that, he joined the queue like the rest of us, and waited patiently for his turn.

Another time, I was in a phone shop with a friend.

She had returned a few years before me. There were two distinct lines facing the two Customer Services staff. There was no one to ask which line to join, so everyone who entered picked one at random. When one of the staff became free there was a moment's hesitation from the two people at the front of the queue. Did each staff deal with the same thing or did each do something different? For the two lines only made sense if each staff member dealt with something different.

It eventually transpired that each did not, to the chagrin of one of the customers. He had been waiting when another person came in and happened to join what turned out be the faster line. He started to quarrel, loudly, 'This is stupid. If each of you does the same thing, you should have only one line. I have been waiting for twenty minutes and that man just came in.'

Another person at the back of the line agreed, 'Yes. You ever been to the airport? When you are checking in, they have one line. It doesn't matter how many people come they have to join the one line, and when someone becomes available the next in line goes. Simple! Your line should be like that.'

One of the Customer Services staff made the mistake of trying to justify the unjustifiable. 'Everyone is supposed to look when they come in to see who is in front of him, and then let that person go first.'

Her remark sent everyone into a rage; talking at once, accusing her of being stupid, and more besides.

'That is the most ignorant thing I have ever heard,' one said. 'When I join a line all, I should have to think about is when I will get to the front.'

'Yes, I agree, I should not have to look across to see whether someone else has been there first. That is idiocy!' another said.

There was a loud and bellicose free-for-all, with almost everyone having a say about the stupidity of the shop's queuing system. To my astonishment, my returnee friend also joined in, telling the staff to remove the rope that formed the two lines, as it was clearly causing confusion.

The two security guards in the shop continued at their post, paying no attention. The customer services staff, outnumbered and defeated, had the good sense now to keep their heads down and to get on serving the customers in front of them.

Eventually, the quarrel petered out. The customers continued queuing in the two lines, still not sure whose turn was next.

30 THE TITLE IS IN MY NAME

TD and Cee, her husband, have thirteen children.
They started young, got married after they had the first
two children, and left for England with them when the
second child was four years old.

TD had a child, or the two pairs of twins, every
eighteen months until she secretly had her tubes tied,
as she put it. Each time she had suggested they
stopped, Cee quoted two scriptures from the Bible.

'Like arrows in the hand of a warrior, so are the
children of one's youth. How blessed is the man whose
quiver is full of them; they will not be ashamed when
they speak with their enemies in the gate.'

And, 'Your wife will be like a fruitful vine within
your house; your children will be like olive shoots
around your table.'

Not that Cee was particularly religious; he had stopped going to church soon after arriving in England. He could hardly fit anything else in after working the long shifts he did; that was the initial excuse. After that many more excuses followed, mainly laced with words such as hypocrisy, foolishness and brainwashing.

TD continued to work in between new-borns finding mainly cleaning jobs from the time each was six weeks old until six weeks before the next birth.

When they were too young to be alone, she went cleaning when Cee was in the house grabbing a few hours' sleep between his various shifts. Later, the older ones minded the younger ones, and she could leave them as soon as they returned from school. She could fit up to six hours in then, starting early evening and finishing in time to get the midnight bus home.

They worked together, she and Cee. They bought a large Victorian house, where only two children had to share a bedroom, and with two large living rooms, a separate dining room and a kitchen. They had a garden too, and they lived near the Common, so the children were never short of space to run and play.

When other people realised, there were thirteen of them in their family they could hardly believe it. The children appeared well cared for and well-adjusted within their large family.

The children did fairly well in school too, with the majority of them going to college to learn a trade, and a few going to good universities.

When they were all out of school and were either married and in their own homes, working or in college or university, TD and Cee finally had enough money to travel to Jamaica. At first, they went together, every two years or so. Then Cee started going in the intervening year alone. He had caught the bug and lived the eleven months when he was in England for the month he would spend in Jamaica.

When only a few of the children remained in full-time education, he suggested to TD that they should start planning to return home for good. TD said she was not ready and needed to see all the children settled in a job. When the children were all settled in their jobs, he raised the subject again. She wanted to see them all married, or settled with a partner. Then she wanted to see the grandchildren born. Then she wanted to be there to be with the grandchildren.

Cee wanted to buy land and build a house in the meantime. TD agreed to the land but not to the building.

Not yet, she said. She needed to have spare money to help the children, just in case. She could see tiny cracks appearing in the marriages and relationships of one or two of the children. She needed to be around for them.

Cee's trips to his beloved Jamaica continued. TD noticed that he had become more secretive and did not return from his trips as effusive as he had been when he used to go with her. She got tired of his one-word answers and stopped asking him anything about his trips.

She started getting her pension, and after a couple of years so did he. His lump sum payment was particularly significant. He had worked for the same company for over forty years. When the money cleared in his account, he handed her a cheque for half of it. She was surprised. There was no need for that she said; he should just put it in their joint saving account. Money had never been one of their bugbears.

There were many little things to disagree about over the years, but they had always agreed about how to spend money; their mortgage and bills, the children. Spending wisely, and saving. They always discussed any major expenditure.

'So why are you giving me half? I don't need anything now. You know I got mine three years ago, and I haven't had cause to touch it yet.'

'That's yours,' he said. 'Yours is yours. I want to give you half of mine. But I'm asking you to let me spend the rest of mine how I want to.'

'So how you want to spend it?" she said, puzzled.

'I am going to use the best part of it to build a little house in Jamaica, and the rest to furnish it.'

'Oh,' she said. 'Oh. When did you decide that? Where is this house going to be? Who is going to supervise the building for you, and take care of it when it's finished and you are not there?'

He rocked his body from side to side but did not answer any of her questions. 'Let's leave it. I gave you your share. You don't need to know the ins and outs about mine,' he said finally.

TD wanted to talk about it some more. She knew something was different about him, that there was a change in him; but she could not put her finger on it. She knew if she pushed him he would clam up even more. She would use her practised tactic and get it out of him little by little, when he was least aware of what she was doing. That strategy has never failed.

But months passed and there was no advance in her knowledge. In the meantime, she was basking in her discovery of European cities in what she called her old age and told him that rather than going to Jamaica, which she knew, she would go to a different city that she did not know each year. TD formed a travel group with women in her church. They looked out for cheap flights, or coach trips, first once then twice a year. Her children were taken aback at first, then full of admiration, treating her to trips for her birthday, their anniversary and Mother's Day. Her retirement was better than she had ever dreamed it could be when children had clung to her legs, and every penny had to be accounted for.

Some months later, Cee told her the house was finished, totally furnished with everything it needed, and he would be spending a few months there every year from then on.

'Oh, that is good,' TD said, genuinely pleased for him. 'That is good. Do you want me to come out and spend a few weeks in it with you?'

'No!' Cee said, too sharply.

'OK. OK. When you ready to show me I will go with you. I'm glad for you, though. I know you want your little place there that you can go to when you ready. It will be good for the children too. They won't have to spend all their time in hotels when they visit. That is good.'

'The children won't want to stay there. It is in the country and only has three bedrooms and no swimming pool. You know they like to be in hotels by the sea, where they can swim and relax. No, the little house won't be the place for them.'

'I see. I see. It is in the country area then?' That was news to her.

He was right; her children would not want to be in the country area with its random, unpredictable water supply, bad roads and frequent power cuts. That was not how they would want to spend their two weeks' holidays.

TD drove him to the airport and waved as he seemed to skip light-footed through passport control.

She was used to him going and did not really miss him. But the house felt twice as big without him. Even when he was there, it seemed far too big for them. But they had decided they could never sell it. Not a day passed when one or more of them did not drop by, children or grandchildren. More often than not one of the grandchildren slept over or came for the weekend.

At least once a year, maybe at Christmas, on one of their birthdays or on an especially hot summer's day, the house would be overrun with everyone. No, they would not sell, they had decided. They needed to have room for everyone. When they died, the children could do what they wanted; sell and each gets his or her share or keep it as it was now, a place for each to be.

TD had planned a two week trip to Lisbon, one of her favourite cities, to coincide with part of his time away. She left the day after he went.

When TD returned home from her trip, it was night and she noticed from outside that the light in their bedroom was on.

She knew she could not have left it on, and even if she had, one of the children would have noticed and turned it off when they dropped by. Perhaps there was a burglary in progress. She called her eldest, JD, who lived on the next road. 'Daddy is home,' she said.

'How you mean he's home? He has come back? Is he sick?'

'No, I don't think so. Go and talk to him.'

Cee was sitting up in bed when she entered the room. She had barely put her bag down when he started talking. There were tears too. She had only seen him cry thirteen times in the fifty-odd years she had known him, and those were when he held each of their children for the first time.

'I am a stupid old man. I know you might not forgive me. I know you might even drive me out.' TD lowered herself onto the edge of the bed, perplexed.

'I met the young woman when I went out there one of the times on my own. She is the daughter of someone I went to primary school with. Yes, I know, she is younger than JD.' Cee said studying his wife's face.

'I thought we loved each other. I sent the money for her to buy the land and asked her to look after building the house. She managed that and got everything done in good time.

'She cleared all the furniture I sent through customs and told me everything was ready.

'When I left two weeks ago, I was not going for three months, I was leaving you to go and live with her. I was going for good. I was going to surprise her, and I couldn't bring myself to tell you. I planned to write a letter after the three months.

'When I got there, she was on the veranda with a man. I thought it was one of her brothers. I called to her to open the gate and let the taxi through with the bags. She left the man on the veranda and came to the gate. She had the gate remote control in her hand but spoke to me through the gate. Imagine it, through my gate that my pension money bought. She spoke to me like I was a common suspect thief.

'She showed me her ring, said she was married now, to her last child's baby father. Last child! I didn't even know she had children. She had told me she didn't have children, and she couldn't wait for us to have children together. She had saved that for the right man, she said.

'She wouldn't as much as open the gate. The man came to the gate and stood laughing, calling me old man, idiot, looking down at my private area and calling me deaders, meaning me impotent and no good to women, telling me to move away from their property.

'I had got there late and the to-ing and fro-ing went on almost all night. I was telling them, even begging them as the night wore on, to open the gate. I needed to rest after the flight. I was hungry too.

'The taxi man left my things on the road. He had to go back to the airport, he said. Children came out on my veranda and stood gawking through the burglar bars, as if they were watching an animal in a zoo.

'The other people from the district came and stood around. I was born and brought up there, and they did not stand up for me. Most of them were laughing and mocking me. They must have known all along, all the time I visited and took them things. I gave them money. I paid for many of their children's school uniform and books over the years. At one time, when night had come, I glimpsed the woman's mother at the window of my house, but she didn't come out. She only pushed something through the window to her daughter.

I called the police in the end and tried to explain to them that it is my land and house. That it was my money that built the house; that my name was on the Title.

She told them that that I was liar. She told them that I had given her money to buy the land and sent her the money as a gift to build the house. She gave the police the paper her mother had pushed through the window. 'See here,' she said, 'It is only my name on the Land Title. The Title is in my name.' 'The police took pity on me and kept me in one of their cells for the rest of the night. There was nowhere else to go.'

Cee stared vacantly at his wife. 'I came back because the Title is in her name.'

ABOUT THE AUTHOR

Vernella Fuller was born in Saint Catherine, Jamaica, in 1956. She is the second eldest of six siblings. Her parents immigrated to England in the early 1960s, and she joined them in 1968. During those early years, Vernella was heavily influenced by her mother, Delceta, and her Grandmother Beatrice, both of whom instilled in her a great love for books, reading, and learning.

Vernella attended secondary school in South London and received an undergraduate degree from University of Sussex; a post-graduate teacher certificate from Goldsmiths, University of London; and masters and doctorate degrees from the Institute of Education, University College London.

Vernella taught history and sociology in secondary school and at the college level in London for over seventeen years. She was and remains an educator and advocate for learning and literacy. In the 1990s, she began writing stories and authoring books about the lives of people with British-Jamaican heritage.

In 2007, Vernella permanently returned to Jamaica. She lives in Rose Hall, Saint James.

Also by Vernella Fuller:
Going Back Home
Unlike Normal Women
Fettered Love: Stories of Courage

www.ingramcontent.com/pod-product-compliance
Lightning Source LLC
Chambersburg PA
CBHW070500260626
47161CB00004B/1384

* 9 7 8 9 7 6 9 5 9 1 1 2 7 *